The Hero Next Door
Irene Hannon

Steeple
Hill®

Published by Steeple Hill Books™

STEEPLE HILL BOOKS

Steeple
Hill®

Recycling programs
for this product may
not exist in your area.

ISBN-13: 978-0-373-81419-0

THE HERO NEXT DOOR

www.SteepleHill.com

Printed in U.S.A.

"This ~~is~~ **ket is safe. You scared me to death! Is that a gun in your hand?"**
Heather asked.

"Yes, and crime happens everywhere,"
J.C. responded.

"The noise we heard is probably feral cats.
I caught them rooting through my trash a few
days ago."

J.C. took a quick look around her backyard and
confirmed that two cats had indeed stuck their
noses in the trash bin.

"Sorry to raise an unnecessary alarm," he said.

"You must travel in rough circles."

In Heather Anderson's world, cats were the
biggest predators on the street.

He, on the other hand, had spent his career
dealing with lowlifes. And he'd been doing it for
so long he didn't know how to behave around a
woman who was untouched by the raw side of
life.

"Well, thanks again." Turning, she disappeared
through her back door.

Suddenly, an odd sensation settled in J.C.'s chest.
One that had nothing to do with the guilt he'd
been carrying for the last month. This was related
to a woman with beautiful hazel eyes.

Books by Irene Hannon

Love Inspired

*Home for the Holidays
*A Groom of Her Own
*A Family to Call Her Own
It Had to Be You
One Special Christmas
The Way Home
Never Say Goodbye
Crossroads

*Vows
**Sisters & Brides
†Heartland Homecomings
††Lighthouse Lane

**The Best Gift
**Gift from the Heart
**The Unexpected Gift
All Our Tomorrows
The Family Man
Rainbow's End
†From This Day Forward
†A Dream To Share
†Where Love Abides
Apprentice Father
††Tides of Hope
††The Hero Next Door

IRENE HANNON

Irene Hannon, who writes both romance and romantic suspense, is an author of more than twenty-five novels. Her books have been honored with both a coveted RITA® Award from Romance Writers of America (the "Oscar" of romantic fiction) and a Reviewers' Choice Award from *Romantic Times BOOKreviews* magazine. More than a million copies of her novels have been sold worldwide.

A former corporate communications executive with a Fortune 500 company, Irene now writes full-time. In her spare time, she enjoys singing, long walks, cooking, gardening and spending time with family. She and her husband make their home in Missouri.

For more information about her and her books, Irene invites you to visit her Web site at www.irenehannon.com.

Love never fails.
   —I Corinthians 13:8

To my husband, Tom—
who is just my cup of tea!

Acknowledgment

Special thanks to Chief William J. Pittman,
Nantucket Police Department,
for his generous assistance.

Chapter One

Justin Clay had always considered June 1 to be the true beginning of summer. The day that marked the transition from cold and dark to warm and bright.

And on this June 1, as the ferry from Hyannis churned into Nantucket Harbor under cloudless blue skies, he hoped that was as true for his life as it was for the weather.

Forearms resting on the railing, he took in the view as the ferry rounded diminutive Brant Point Light and the Coast Guard station. Boats of every type and size dotted the blue water below the tree-filled town, which perched on a gentle hillside in the background. The gold dome of a clock tower and a tall white steeple soared over the leafy branches, while weathered gray clapboard buildings with white trim predominated along the waterfront.

Lifting his face to the warmth of the sun, Justin took

a deep breath. He'd wanted a complete change of scene, and this qualified. The tranquil, pristine vista felt a world removed from the violent, gritty back-streets of Chicago he frequented. Perhaps here, twenty-six miles from the mainland, on this fourteen-by-three-and-a-half-mile speck of land in the Atlantic Ocean, he would find release from the pain and guilt that gnawed at his soul.

As the ferry eased beside the wharf, Justin picked up his oversize duffel bag, slung his backpack over one shoulder and sent a silent prayer heavenward that when he boarded this boat again in three months to head home, he'd be leaving a lot of baggage behind.

Sliding a tray of mini-scones onto the cooling rack on the stainless-steel prep table, Heather Anderson checked the clock. 1:10 p.m. In less than an hour, thirty-four customers would be arriving for a proper British high tea.

Where was Julie?

As she cast a worried glance out the window, the gate by the garage swung open to admit her assistant, and Heather released a relieved breath. The Devon Rose might be a one-woman show for most of the day, but she needed help with the actual serving.

Pushing through the back door, her white blouse and black skirt immaculate even if her French braid was slightly askew, Julie sent her an apologetic look. "Sorry. I had a flat tire."

"No problem. I'm just glad you're here." Heather adjusted the oven temperature, strode over to the commercial-size refrigerator and pulled out a tray of mini-quiches. "Did Todd change it for you?"

"Yes. But I hated to wake him." Julie began arranging the scones on the second level of the three-tiered silver serving stands lined up on the counter, tucking flowers among them. "There was some kind of drug incident in the wee hours of the morning, and he was beat when he got home. But he didn't complain about the tire."

"And you've been married how long? Twenty years?" Heather shook her head as she took the lids off fifteen teapots in a variety of styles and arranged them on a long counter. "He's one in a million, Julie. Count your blessings."

"I do. Every day. But there are other good guys out there, too, you know." She sent Heather a meaningful glance.

"Maybe." Heather slid the quiches into the oven. "But they're few and far between. And based on past experience, not likely to come calling at my door. I'd have to beat the bushes to find one." She closed the oven door and turned to Julie. "And as far as I'm concerned, it's not worth the effort."

Justin hoisted his backpack into a more comfortable position, pulled the Nantucket town map out of the back pocket of his jeans and perused the maze of streets. In one more block he'd be at Lighthouse Lane—and the cottage he'd be calling home for the next three months.

Refolding the map, he shoved it back into his pocket, hefted his duffel bag and continued down the sidewalk. As he'd already discovered on his trek from the wharf, unlike the dirty, decaying back alleys of Chicago, Nantucket was clean and well kept. The people he'd passed, many on bicycles, had been dressed nicely, and they'd smiled at him. A welcome change of pace from the suspicious looks he was used to, cast by questionable characters as they slunk into dark doorways.

Nantucket wasn't crime free, Justin knew. But he doubted he'd have to worry about double crosses here—or mistakes that could snuff out lives.

A lump rose in his throat, and he paused at the corner of Lighthouse Lane to blink away the sudden film of moisture that blurred his vision. With memories so fresh and raw, maybe coming to Nantucket hadn't been such a good idea, after all. Maybe he should have used the last three months of his four-month leave to veg. Rent a cabin in the woods and disappear. Or borrow a boat and hang out on Lake Michigan.

Yet prayer had led him here, back to his roots as a beat cop. He'd asked the Lord to help him find answers—and direction. To give him some quiet time to work through the issues that weighed him down. So this summer job opportunity had seemed providential.

Things would be better here.

They had to be.

Crossing the street, he turned left onto Lighthouse Lane. His landlady, Edith Shaw, had said hers was the third—and last—house on the right, and he had no trouble spotting the Federal-style home she'd described.

But far more impressive was the two-story structure on the corner. Constructed of clapboard, like the Shaw house, but painted white instead of yellow, it featured black shutters. Thanks to a Greek Revival roofline with a deep frieze—along with a small, elevated, white-pillared front porch—it had a grand, stately air. A discreet sign beside the door said The Devon Rose.

Squinting, Justin could just make out the elaborate script below the name: *Serving Wednesday through Sunday.* Sounded like a restaurant. And mere steps away from his new digs. Pretty convenient. Once he dropped his bags off at his cottage, he might come back here for a quick bite to tide him over until he stocked his kitchen.

His stomach growled, and taking the cue, he picked up his pace, passing a snug, weathered clapboard cottage with sage-colored trim that was sandwiched on a shallow lot between The Devon Rose and the Shaw house. The backyards of the two larger houses must adjoin in the rear, he concluded.

Continuing to Edith Shaw's house, he found an envelope bearing his name taped beside the doorbell. The note inside directed him through the gate in the tall privet hedge to a spacious private backyard. From there he followed a flagstone path across the thick carpet of grass to the cottage, which was surrounded by budding hydrangea bushes. It was tucked into the back corner, separated from The Devon Rose property only by the privet hedge.

As he'd been warned, the structure was small. But that was okay; he didn't require a lot of square footage. At six-one, however, he considered headroom important. He hoped the compact accommodations wouldn't be too claustrophobic.

Much to his relief, when he stepped inside, he realized the outward appearance had been deceptive. Or perhaps the sense of spaciousness was due to the vaulted ceiling. A queen-size bed stood in the far left corner of the room, while a small couch upholstered in hydrangea-print fabric stood against the wall to the left of the front door, a brass reading lamp beside it. An old chest, topped with a glass bowl of hard candy, served as a coffee table.

In the tiny kitchenette to the right, a wooden café table was flanked by matching chairs with blue-and-yellow plaid seat cushions. A quick peek confirmed that the bath was behind the kitchen. No tub, but a decent-size shower, Jason noted.

Setting his luggage on the polished pine floor, he spotted a plate of what appeared to be homemade pumpkin bread in the middle of the café table.

His stomach growled again and, stripping off the

plastic wrap, Justin devoured one of the slices. But it barely put a dent in his appetite. He needed real food.

Rewrapping the plate of sweet bread, he freshened up and headed back out the door to the closest restaurant.

The Devon Rose.

"Table six asked for more scones. And nine wants a refill of Earl Grey." Julie swept into the kitchen carrying a china teapot.

Heather arranged three more scones on a small serving plate. "I'll deliver these if you'll handle the Earl."

"Will do." Julie headed toward the shelves above the counter, where an array of canisters held white, black, green, oolong and herbal teas.

Plate of scones in hand, Heather pushed through the swinging door into the dining room. As she emerged from behind the ornate wooden grill that blocked patrons' views into the more functional areas of the house, the calm oasis of The Devon Rose soothed her, as always. Soft classical music provided a genteel backdrop to the muted conversation and tinkle of silver spoons against fine china cups. Silk draperies at the tall windows and crisp white linen tablecloths helped absorb the echo produced by the ten-foot ceilings, marble mantels and polished hardwood floors in the three rooms where tea was served.

Here in the original dining room, a century-old hand-painted mural of a Tudor garden lent a touch of elegance. Her great aunt's antique mahogany table still stood under an ornate crystal chandelier and accommodated larger groups for special occasions. Today it was set for eight, and Heather stopped to exchange a few words with the guest of honor, who was celebrating her eightieth birthday.

Crossing the foyer, with its elaborate stairway that hugged the wall as it wound up to the second floor, Heather passed through an arched doorway into twin parlors connected by open pocket doors. Intimate tables for two lined the walls of both rooms, with a table for four in the center of each. Table six was beside the mantel on the far wall.

"I understand I have some scone lovers here." With a smile, she set the plate on the pristine linen, checking to confirm that the couple had a sufficient quantity of wild strawberry jam and the clotted cream she imported from Devon.

"My dear, they're divine! Just like the ones we had in Cornwall last year," the older woman gushed.

"Mighty fine," her companion seconded as he reached for one of the scones.

Heather made a leisurely circuit of the room, exchanging a few words with the customers at each table. As usual, she had a full house. Tea was by reservation only, and she was often booked weeks in advance. It was rare to have a no-show.

Today, however, table four was the exception to

that rule. A tourist reservation, Heather assumed as she passed it on her way to the foyer. Visitors to the island often changed their plans on a whim. That was one of the reasons she preferred her local clientele.

The front door swung open as she exited the parlor, and she stopped in surprise. Tea began at two, and it was well past that now. Perhaps tardy arrivals for table four?

But the tall, dark-haired man who stepped into the foyer was alone. Attired in jeans and a long-sleeved black shirt, he was nothing like her typical male customers—older men accompanying their wives. This guy was in his midthirties, she estimated—and very masculine. With brown eyes so dark they could pass for black, he was well built and radiated an intense, ready-for-action energy.

The tranquil mood in the tearoom suddenly shifted. The clatter of spoons and forks ceased, and an expectant hush replaced the quiet conversation.

If the man who'd crossed her threshold noticed the newly charged atmosphere, he didn't let on. Instead, he closed the door behind him and gave Heather a swift scan. She had a feeling he missed nothing—from her black leather pumps and slim black skirt to her short-sleeved silk blouse, her single strand of pearls and the tortoiseshell barrette that restrained her shoulder-length light brown hair at her nape.

She'd call the look practiced, except that implied ogling. His sweep felt almost…professional. Automatic. As if he were accustomed to assessing everyone he met.

When the silence lengthened, she arched an eyebrow. "May I help you?"

"I was hoping to get some lunch." One corner of his mouth hitched up into an appealing half smile.

To Heather's annoyance, her pulse accelerated. "I'm afraid we serve afternoon tea, not lunch."

He surveyed the dining room, giving her an excellent view of the chiseled planes of his face and the strong line of his jaw. All the women watching him seemed to smile in unison, Heather noted.

"I suppose I'm not dressed for a fancy place like this. But I'm hungry, and this was the closest spot serving food." Facing her again, his half smile edged up a notch. "I'm staying in Edith Shaw's cottage for the summer, and I just arrived on the ferry. I'm Justin Clay, by the way. J.C. to my friends." He held out his hand.

The police officer from Chicago, Heather realized as she moved forward. Edith had mentioned him.

At five foot six, she didn't think of herself as short, but she had to tip her head back to return his greeting. "Heather Anderson."

His warm, lean fingers closed over hers in a strong grip, and her breath got stuck in her throat. Talk about good-looking! Yet at close range, she couldn't help noticing fine lines radiating from the corners of his eyes, as well as fatigue in their depths. Both projected a soul-deep weariness that went way beyond physical tiredness.

Her conscience pricking, Heather wavered. She couldn't send him away hungry. Not when he was a neighbor—and she had an empty table. "You're welcome to stay, if tea fare will be sufficient."

The other side of his mouth hitched up to form a complete smile, and his fingers tightened for an instant before he released her hand. "I'm sure it will be fine."

Telling her heart to behave, Heather led the way to table four. "In general, we're fully booked. This was a rare no-show."

"My lucky day, I guess."

She turned to find him watching her. With some men, Heather might have interpreted that comment as a come-on. With this one, she wasn't certain. His neutral expression told her nothing. Nor did his eyes reveal the motivation behind his remark. It was as if he'd had a lot of practice masking his emotions.

"What sort of tea would you like?" She plucked a printed list of offerings out of a small silver holder on the table and handed it to him.

After a cursory scan, he passed it back. "What are the chances I could get a cup of coffee?"

She gave him a bemused look. "In a tearoom? None, I'm afraid. Sorry."

"Okay. Then I'll take your strongest tea."

Assam, she decided at once. It was full-bodied,

robust and malty. They didn't have many takers for that potent brew. But she figured he could handle it.

"I think we have one you'll like. Your food will be out in a few minutes."

"Thanks."

Turning, Heather crossed the room toward the foyer. She was tempted to check and see if Justin Clay was still watching her, but she squelched that silly impulse. Why should she care?

Yet as she passed the front door, she couldn't help recalling what she'd told Julie a couple of hours ago, about good guys being few and far between—and not likely to come calling at her door.

She didn't know a thing about the man who'd just arrived, except that he seemed out of place in The Devon Rose. But intuition told her he might fall into the good-guy camp.

Of course, her intuition had failed her before, with her old boyfriend Mark. As had her mother's, with Heather's unfaithful father. As had her sister Susan's, with her philandering husband. All of those examples reinforced the sad truth—the Anderson women had no luck when it came to men.

So while Justin Clay might, indeed, be a good guy, Heather didn't intend to find out.

Because she didn't trust her judgment when it came to the opposite sex.

And there was no way she'd risk putting her heart in jeopardy ever again. No matter how appealing the man.

Chapter Two

J.C. swirled his last French fry in the generous dollop of ketchup on his plate and popped it in his mouth. The fries and the burger had been the perfect chaser to his afternoon tea, which had done little more than take the edge off his hunger.

Not that he had any complaints about the food at the swanky tearoom. Those little puffy dough things filled with chicken salad had been tasty. The quiche had been okay. As for those little scones with jam and that cream stuff—he could have eaten a dozen of them. And every one of the five desserts had been amazing.

It was the amount, not the flavor, of the food that had sent him in hot pursuit of the nearest restaurant the instant he'd stepped out the door of The Devon Rose. None of the items on that three-tiered contraption had been bigger than a sausage patty.

And the bill had been a shocker. He calculated

that his foray into the world of high tea had cost him close to two bucks a bite.

Wiping his mouth on a napkin, J.C. leaned back in his seat. In fairness, the prices were on the high side in this establishment, too. He wasn't used to twelve-dollar hamburgers. At this rate, he'd eat up his first month's salary in a week. A trip to the grocery store was high on his agenda for tomorrow, after he had breakfast with his new boss—and Chicago PD alumnus—Adam Burke.

As for the cost of the tea—he didn't regret the budget-straining expense. It had been a unique experience, in an atmosphere he could only describe as elegant.

A word that fit the owner as well.

Taking a sip of coffee, he thought about Heather Anderson. Now there was a lady. From her every-hair-in-place wispy bangs, to her graceful, ringless fingers as she'd poured his tea, to her classy attire, she'd oozed culture and refinement.

In other words, she was way out of his league.

Not that it mattered. His priorities for his stay on Nantucket didn't include a relationship. He had enough to deal with without adding romance to the mix.

Draining his mug, he pulled some bills from his wallet and tossed them on the table. Before the day ended, he had several more things to do—and thinking about the lovely tearoom owner wasn't on his list.

Yet try as he might, he couldn't stop images of her from floating through his mind as he strolled down the cobblestone street and veered off toward Lighthouse Lane.

"Knock, knock. Anyone home?"

Wiping her hands on a towel, Heather smiled at the stout older woman who stood on the other side of her screen door. Since Edith and Chester Shaw had retired to Nantucket eleven years ago, the couple had become like family to her.

"Come on in." Heather reached for the two leftover scones, added a generous portion of clotted cream and strawberry jam to the plate, and edged it toward Edith. "Help yourself if you're hungry."

"Oh, my. I shouldn't." Her neighbor cast a longing glance at the offering. Then, with a shrug, she pulled a stool up to the stainless-steel prep table and slathered the scones with jam and cream. "But these are impossible to resist, as you well know."

Chuckling, Heather continued measuring ingredients for the chocolate tarts that would grace tomorrow's three-tiered servers. "What's up?"

"Did you notice any activity at my place while Chester and I were away? The note's gone from my front door, so I know my tenant arrived. I'd planned to invite him to dinner since he doesn't know a soul here other than Burke, but I'm afraid he may already have gone out to get a bite."

Julie pushed through the door from the dining

room. "Hi, Edith. Heather, I set the tables for tomorrow and refilled the sugar bowls. Anything else before I take off?"

"That should do it, thanks. To answer your question, Edith, he stopped in here around three in search of food. He thought we served lunch." Heather stirred the chocolate in the double boiler. "I assumed he went back to your place when he left."

"No one answered my knock. How long was he here?"

"He stayed for tea," Julie offered, retrieving her purse and sweater from a chair and heading for the door.

Edith arched an eyebrow.

"I think he liked what we had to offer," Julie added.

Heather turned in time to see her assistant wink at Edith and incline her head toward her employer before pushing through the door.

As it banged shut behind her, Edith tipped her head and appraised Heather. "So Justin Clay stayed for tea."

Heather shot her a warning look. "Don't make anything out of this, Edith."

"What's there to make anything out of?" She took a bite of her second scone. "I haven't met Mr. Clay, but I understand from Burke that he's got quite a reputation on the Chicago force for some pretty high-stakes undercover work. I sort of pictured him as the tall, muscular, rugged type. I guess I'm having a little trouble imagining him holding a dainty teacup and eating finger sandwiches. Unless he had an ulterior motive."

Planting her hands on her hips, Heather narrowed her eyes. "Just because you had a hand in getting Kate and Craig together doesn't give you the right to work on my love life, Edith." Charter fishing boat captain Kate MacDonald, who occupied the little cottage between her house and Edith's, had recently married Nantucket's Coast Guard commander, and Heather knew Edith was proud of her role as matchmaker.

"How can I work on something that doesn't exist?"

"Very funny."

"No. Very true. And sad."

"You know I'm not in the market for romance, Edith. And you know why."

"Not all men are like your father. Or Mark."

Removing the melted chocolate from the stove, Heather poured it into a mixing bowl containing the remaining ingredients for the filling and began to stir. Even after two years, the mere mention of the dashing Boston hotel executive who'd come to the island to manage a collection of boutique properties—and who'd finagled his way past her defenses—left a bitter taste in her mouth.

"I agree, Edith. But the Anderson women always seem to pick losers."

"Humph." The older woman licked a speck of

cream off her finger. "What does the island's newest police officer look like?"

"Dark hair, dark eyes, six-one or two." Heather began scooping the filling into the miniature tart shells.

"As in tall, dark and handsome?"

"I didn't say handsome."

"You mean he's ugly?"

As a mental image of her unexpected customer flashed across her mind, Heather lost her methodical scooping rhythm and a ball of filling plopped onto the stainless-steel counter. Expelling an irritated breath, she gritted her teeth and swiped it up. "He's not ugly."

"Well, I'm anxious to meet him. I already like his name. Justin Clay. It sounds very strong and masculine."

"He goes by J.C."

"Oh? How do you know?"

She was in too deep now to do anything but tell the truth, Heather realized, regretting the slip. "When he introduced himself, he said that's what his friends call him."

"His *friends.*" Edith mulled that over as she slid off the stool. Ambling toward the back porch, she tossed one parting comment over her shoulder. "Well, that's a start." Without waiting for a response, she pushed through the door and disappeared down the steps.

Dismayed, Heather blew out a breath and shook her head. She'd seen that look in Edith's eyes before, and she knew what it meant—the older woman was in matchmaking mode. Now that Kate and Craig had tied the knot, she was on the prowl for new victims.

Meaning J.C. would probably end up ruing the day he'd stepped into The Devon Rose.

"Marci, it's J.C."

"Hey, big brother. You arrived safe and sound, I assume."

"Yep." He stretched out on the bed in his new digs, testing the mattress. Nice and firm. Just the way he liked it.

"So how's life on a ritzy island?"

"I haven't seen the ritzy parts yet. But I did have a ritzy experience today. I went to tea."

Her response was preceded by several beats of silence. "You hate tea."

"The food was good," J.C. countered. "You would have liked it, Marci. White tablecloths, classical music, flowers."

"You hate tea."

"You already said that."

"I know. I'm trying to make sense of this. What on earth prompted you to go to tea?"

An elegant, graceful woman with hazel eyes.

As that thought echoed in his mind, J.C. frowned. He wished he could attribute his foray into that civilized ritual to hunger, but he couldn't dispute the truth. Had it not been for Heather Anderson's quiet loveliness and refinement, he would have vacated the rarified atmosphere of The Devon Rose in a heartbeat, no matter how loudly his stomach protested.

"The question wasn't that hard, J.C."

At Marci's wry prompt, he pulled himself back to the present. "I was hungry. And the tea place is next door to my cottage. Anyway, it's nice here. Quiet."

"Good. Maybe you'll sleep better."

"I slept okay in Chicago."

"Hey, you don't have to pretend with me. I'm your sister, okay? I know you've been through hell this past month. So rest. Relax. Think. And move on."

"It's not that easy."

"I know." Her words came out scratchy, and she cleared her throat. "Pray some more to that God of yours. Maybe He'll come through for you if you keep bending His ear."

"I intend to. And He's your God, too, Marci. I wish you and Nathan would give Him a chance."

"You don't need to worry about me. I can take care of myself. As for Nathan…he's a lost cause. Do you still write to him every week?"

"Yes."

"I doubt he even reads the letters."

"Maybe not. But he gets them. And knows I'm thinking about him."

"Talk about a wasted life." Disgust laced her words.

"It's not too late for him to turn things around." J.C. tried to sound optimistic as he stared at the ceiling, but in truth, his hope was dimming. His younger brother's bitterness hadn't abated one iota since the day eight years ago when he'd been sentenced to a decade behind bars for armed robbery.

"Give it up, J.C. All those trips you made down to Pontiac… What good did they do? Most of the time he wouldn't even talk to you. He doesn't like cops."

"I was his brother first, Marci. And I have to try."

"Yeah. I know." Her words grew softer. "Too bad you were saddled with two reprobates for siblings."

There was a hint of humor in her voice, but J.C. knew how she'd struggled with self-image. And hated that deep inside, for reasons he'd never been able to fathom, she might continue to feel less than worthy. "I don't think of you that way, Marci. And neither does anyone else. You've done great." Then he lightened his tone, knowing praise made her uncomfortable. "I'm impressed with that big word, by the way. Reprobate, huh? All that schooling you're getting must be paying off."

"Very funny."

A knock sounded at his door, and he swung his legs to the floor. "Someone's come calling, kiddo. Gotta run."

"Okay, bro. Take care and don't be a stranger."

As the line went dead, J.C. stood and slipped his cell phone into his pocket. Smoothing down the back of his hair with one hand, he opened the door with the other.

"You must be Justin. Or J.C., as I'm told you prefer to be called. You're just the way Heather described you. Welcome to Nantucket. I'm Edith Shaw, and this is my husband, Chester." An older woman with short, silvery-gray hair stuck out her hand.

As J.C. returned her firm clasp and leaned forward to grasp her husband's fingers, he gave his landlords a quick once-over.

Edith's blue eyes sparked with interest, radiating energy. Although she wore black slacks and a simple short-sleeved blue blouse, J.C. sensed there was a mischievous streak beneath her conservative attire.

Pink-cheeked Chester, on the other hand, struck him as an aw-shucks kind of guy, content to let his lively wife run the show. He wore grass-stained overalls, suggesting he was a gardener, and a shock of gray hair fell over his forehead. Someone had tried to tame his ornery cowlick, but it had refused to be subdued.

"I'm happy to meet you both." J.C. smiled and gestured toward the inside of the cottage. "This place is perfect. And thank you for the pumpkin bread, Mrs. Shaw."

She waved his thanks aside. "Plenty more where that came from. And it's Edith and Chester. I was going to invite you to dinner, but I understand you've already eaten next door."

J.C. nodded, admiring her investigative skills. "That's right."

"Well, Heather does a fine job. But—" she sized him up "—it's not a lot of food for a full-grown man. You'd be welcome to join us. I guarantee my beef stew will stick to your ribs."

After·consuming the tea goodies, a burger and fries, and the last of Edith's pumpkin bread, there was no way he could eat another meal. "To be honest, I also paid a visit to Arno's."

Chester chuckled. "I'm with you. I like Heather's food just fine, but it's not enough to keep a bird alive."

"Now, Chester," Edith chided. "Heather's a wonderful cook and a great hostess. I'm sure she made you feel welcome, didn't she?"

Her keen look took him off guard. As did the odd undertone, which he couldn't identify. "Yes. She was very hospitable."

She gave him a satisfied smile. "Well, then, I'll bring you out a plate of stew later, and you can put it in the fridge for tomorrow night. And anytime you need anything, you let us know. We're just a holler away."

As she marched across the lawn to her back door, Chester following a step behind, J.C. regarded the stately clapboard house where he'd had tea earlier. Only the roof and parts of the second floor were visible through the trees.

So the tearoom owner had described him to

Edith. Interesting. And intriguing. What had she said? he wondered.

More to the point, however, why should he care?

Looking back toward the Shaw house, he found Edith observing him, her pleased smile still in place. With a wave, she disappeared inside.

Planting his fists on his hips, he studied her closed door. What was that all about?

But considering the glint in her eyes, maybe he didn't want to know.

Chapter Three

❧

"Now that's what I call a breakfast." J.C. sat back in the booth and dropped his napkin beside his plate. "And the price was right. What's the name of this place again?"

"Downyflake. Or, as the locals call it, The Flake." Burke signaled to the waitress. "I'm glad you enjoyed it. You look like you could use a few good meals."

That was true. But until yesterday, his appetite had been nonexistent. "I've been eating well since I've been here. Must be the salt air. And it's been good for you, too. You look younger than when you left Chicago."

Three years ago, when Burke had announced he was taking the chief job on Nantucket, J.C. hadn't been convinced the senior detective would acclimate to the slower pace. He was glad his fears had been unfounded. At fifty-three, Burke's trademark buzz cut might be more salt than pepper, but the tension in his features had eased.

"The life here suits me," Burke confirmed.

"Here you go, Chief." The blond-haired, college-age waitress set the bill on the table, flashed them each a smile and trotted on to the next customer.

When J.C. reached for his wallet, Burke shook his head and picked up the bill. "The first one's on me. Let's go take a tour of the station."

Less than five minutes later, Burke pulled into a parking space in front of an attractive brick building that sported a row of dormer windows.

"Used to be the fire station," Burke told him as he set the brake. "Won't take long to do a walk-through."

Within fifteen minutes J.C. had met the dispatcher on duty—who also served as telephone operator and receptionist. She was ensconced behind a window that looked into the small lobby. The first floor housed the sergeant's office, interview rooms, a five-cell lockup and a juvenile holding cell; upstairs was home to the department's four detectives, a briefing room and a few other staff offices.

At the end of the tour, Burke ushered J.C. into his office. The chief's desk stood in front of the room's single window and faced the door, a credenza on the right and a bookcase on the left. Cream-colored walls brightened the space.

"Quite an improvement over your digs in Chicago." J.C. grinned as he inspected the room.

"No kidding. I not only have walls, I have a window."

"Yeah." J.C. strolled over to peruse the view of nearby businesses. "And if you get hungry for sushi, it's just steps away."

"Hey, don't knock it. There's more to life than greasy burgers and stale donuts. So how's the cottage?"

"It's perfect. Thanks for recommending it. How do you know the Shaws?"

"From church. It's a nice little congregation. You'd be welcome to join us."

"I'll probably take you up on that. I need to find a place to worship while I'm here."

Burke gestured toward the chairs to the left of the door. "Now that you've seen the station, any questions?"

"Not yet."

"How about if I ask a few, then?" Burke closed the door.

J.C. had assumed this was coming. To his credit, Burke hadn't pushed for information when he'd offered him the temporary summer position. But now that J.C. was here, he wasn't surprised Burke wanted more details. Besides, they'd been friends for more than ten years. His interest would be both professional and personal.

Taking one of the chairs, J.C. leaned forward. His breakfast congealed into a cold lump in the pit of his stomach, and he kept his gaze fixed on his clasped hands. "What do you want to know?"

"Relax, J.C." Burke sat and crossed an ankle over a knee. "This isn't an interrogation. It's one friend lending an ear to another. And just so you know, I called Dennis and Ben. *After* I offered you the job."

J.C. jerked his head up. Dennis had been the office supervisor and Ben his street supervisor during his nine-month deep-cover assignment. They knew the details of that fateful night as well as anyone.

"If you talked to them, you know what happened."

"I'd like to hear your side of it."

Rising abruptly, J.C. shoved his hands into the pockets of his jeans and strode back to the window. There were lots of people on the street now. Laughing, smiling, chatting. Everyone seemed to be having a good time.

He turned his back on them.

"It was in the report. I'm sure Dennis would give you a copy."

"I'd rather hear it from you."

J.C. fisted his hands in his pockets. "And I'd rather not talk about it."

The chief pursed his lips. "I'm going to assume the required counseling didn't help a whole lot."

J.C. snorted in disgust. "She didn't have a clue about the stresses of undercover work. The isolation. The no-man's-land existence, pretending to belong one place but cut off from the place you do belong. The strain of putting your life on hold to bring about justice. And that's when things are going well." He took a deep breath and let it out as his shoulders slumped. "But after all that effort, all that sacrifice, to watch two of your buddies take bullets because you made a mistake…" His voice turned to gravel, and he gripped the back of Burke's desk chair.

"According to everything I heard, it wasn't your fault."

"I slipped up somewhere. If I hadn't, Jack and Scott would still be alive. We walked into an ambush, Burke."

"I heard you came pretty close to getting taken out yourself."

J.C. averted his head. "There are days I wish I had been." A fresh wave of anguish swept over him, and a muscle in his jaw clenched. "Or that it had been me instead of them. They each left a wife and young children. No one would have missed me."

In the ensuing silence, J.C.'s words echoed in his mind. If he was in Burke's shoes, he'd be having serious second thoughts about now. No chief wanted a troubled cop on the force. Traumatized people didn't think clearly. They were distracted and emotional, and they often overreacted—or underreacted—to stressful situations. In law enforcement, that could be deadly.

Steeling himself, J.C. faced the older man.

Although he didn't detect any doubt, cops were good at hiding their feelings.

"Did I just shoot myself in the foot?"

Burke cocked his head. "Should I be worried?"

"No. I'll admit I haven't resolved all my issues. But I'm working on them. That's why I asked for an extended leave. I knew I needed some time to regroup in a different environment. Since I started as a beat cop, it felt right to go back to those roots. And after all my years undercover, I know how to compartmentalize. I can promise you I won't let what happened in Chicago compromise my performance here."

As Burke regarded him, J.C. held his breath. It wouldn't be the end of the world if he was sent packing. But in the twenty-four hours he'd been on Nantucket, he'd sensed that this place held the key to a lot of the questions he'd been unable to answer in Chicago. And he didn't want to leave.

"Okay, J.C." Burke stood. "I wouldn't touch most guys in your situation with a ten-foot pole. What you've been through can mess with a person's mind. But I've seen you in a lot of tough situations, and you've always been steady under pressure. From what I've heard and observed, I don't have any reason to think that's changed." He held out his hand. "Welcome to the Nantucket PD."

As J.C. returned Burke's solid clasp, he forced his stiff shoulders to relax. And sent a silent plea to the Lord to stick close.

Because while he was confident his training would kick in should he find himself in a volatile situation, he was counting on the summer being quiet relative to the Chicago crime scene. None of the lawbreaking he was likely to encounter here—petty theft, traffic violations, even drug issues—should involve altercations where lives hung in the balance.

And that was good. He didn't want any more baggage.

What he did want was a quiet, uncomplicated summer that gave him plenty of opportunity to sit on a beach and do some serious thinking about the rest of his life.

The muffled rattling sounded suspicious.

J.C. slowed his pace as he approached the gate leading to the garden beside The Devon Rose. Since his breakfast with Burke, he'd spent the day exploring the town, including an all-important visit to the grocery store. He was ready to call it a night. But he wasn't wired to ignore odd sounds, and this one fell into that category.

Juggling his bags of groceries, he listened. It sounded as if a metal object was being shaken.

In Chicago, following that kind of rattle into a dark alley often led him to a homeless person rooting through a Dumpster or trash can. But as near as he could tell, homeless people were rare on Nantucket.

Thieves were another story. Due to the private backyards, which were often hidden from the street by lush vegetation or privet hedges, burglars could pull off robberies without detection. According to Burke, that was one of the biggest problems in the quiet season, when many vacation homes were vacant.

This wasn't the quiet season, however. Nor did The Devon Rose appear to be vacant. Light from an upper window spilled into the deepening dusk.

Another subtle rattle sounded, and a light was flipped on on the lower level of the house. Heather must have heard the sound, too, and was going out to investigate.

Not a good plan if an intruder was nearby.

A shot of adrenaline sharpened his reflexes, and J.C. set his bags on the sidewalk. Unlike the entrance to Edith's backyard—a rose-covered arbor with a three-foot-high picket gate—Heather had gone the privacy route. Her gate, framed by a tall privet hedge, was six feet high and solid wood. The U-shaped latch, however, provided easy access.

Stepping to one side of the gate, J.C. lifted the latch. To his relief, it moved noiselessly. He opened the gate enough to slip through, shutting it behind him as he melted into the shadows of a nearby bush.

Any other time, J.C. would have admired the precise, geometric pattern of Heather's formal boxwood garden, with its ornate birdbath and beds of colorful flowers that reflected a well-planned symmetry. Instead, he focused on the back of the house, where he expected her to emerge any second—and perhaps step into a dangerous situation.

He heard the door open at the same time the rattling resumed. Both sounds came from the rear. Sprinting down the brick path that bordered her side garden, he crouched at the back corner of the house and stole a look at the porch.

As he'd feared, Heather was standing in clear sight, the porch light spotlighting her.

Providing a perfect target.

Another rattle. Now he could pinpoint the source. It was coming from behind a privet hedge at the back of her property.

Pulling his off-duty snub-nosed .38 revolver from its concealed holster on his belt, he stepped forward as Heather descended the two steps from the porch. She gasped at his sudden appearance, but when he put a finger to his lips and motioned her to join him, she followed his instructions in silence. Taking her arm, he drew her into the shadows beside the house.

As he pressed her against the siding, shielding her body from the rear of the yard, he spoke near her ear. "I was walking by and heard a noise in the back."

"So did I. That's why I came out."

Her whispered breath was warm on his neck, and a faint, pleasing…distracting…floral scent filled his nostrils. "It would have been safer to call the police."

She blinked up at him in the dusky light. "This isn't Chicago. Nantucket is safe. And you scared me to death." She flicked a quick look at his hand. "Is that a gun?"

"Yes. And crime happens everywhere."

"Not in my backyard. The noise we heard is probably feral cats. They're a big problem on the island. I caught them rooting through my trash a few days ago. The cans are inside a wooden box with a heavy lid, but it's not shutting quite right. I think one of the cats must have squeezed in again. Chester's going to fix it one of these days."

Heat crept up the back of J.C.'s neck. If Heather's assumption was correct, he'd pulled his gun on a cat.

Not the most auspicious beginning for his Nantucket law enforcement interlude.

But he'd come this far. He might as well follow through. "I'll check it out, just to be on the safe side. Wait here."

Without giving her a chance to respond, J.C. worked his way to the hedge in back. A quick look around the side confirmed her theory. Two cats had their noses stuck under the slightly opened lid of the trash bin, while a rustling sound came from inside.

At the same time he saw them, the cats got wind of his presence. With amazing speed and agility, the two outside the bin leaped to the ground, bounded toward the privet hedge and dove through. The third scrambled out and followed his friends.

Holstering his gun, J.C. tried to tamp down his embarrassment. Accustomed as he was to finding danger around every corner, the relative safety of Nantucket was obviously going to take some getting used to.

Heather was leaning against one of the back porch posts when he emerged, arms folded across her chest. "I heard them scrambling over the wood. I assumed it was safe to come out."

"Sorry to raise an unnecessary alarm. It was an instinctive reaction."

"You must travel in rough circles."

"Yeah."

"I appreciate the thought, anyway."

Amusement glinted in the depths of her eyes, and J.C. had a feeling she'd have a good chuckle about this later. He could only hope she'd keep the incident to herself. If she told Edith, he suspected half the island would hear about the feral felines' caper within twenty-four hours. Burke had told him his landlord was well-connected and a better source of Nantucket news than the newspapers.

But he'd worry about that later. At the moment, he was too busy enjoying the view. Backlit by the lantern beside the door, Heather's shoulder-length hair hung soft and full, free of restraint, the gold highlights shimmering. The light also silhouetted her willowy frame, which was accentuated by jeans and a soft tank top. Gone were the classy pearls and silk that had made her seem so inaccessible.

He had to remind himself to breathe.

Yet if yesterday he'd felt outclassed in her presence, tonight he found a different reason to keep his distance.

Heather Anderson had never been tainted by exposure to violence. In her world, cats were the biggest predators.

He, on the other hand, had spent his career dealing with the lowlifes of Chicago. And he'd been doing it for so long, he didn't even know how to behave around a woman who was untouched by the raw side of life.

She tucked her hair behind her ear and shifted from one foot to the other. "Well…thanks again."

"No problem."

Turning, she disappeared through the door. Thirty seconds later, the downstairs light was extinguished.

As J.C. retraced his steps to the gate, an odd heaviness settled in his chest. One that had nothing to do with the burden of guilt he'd been carrying for the past month. This was related to a woman with hazel eyes.

Though he knew little about her, J.C. sensed that Heather was a kind, decent, caring person. The sort of woman who would add warmth and sunlight and joy to a man's life.

But not to his.

As appealing as she was, as tempted as he might be to explore the magnetic pull he felt in her presence, in three months he'd be returning to

Chicago. Working the grittiest cases. Dealing with sources in the worst parts of town. Putting his life on the line every single day. And if no one he'd yet dated had had the stomach for that risk long-term, there was no way a woman like Heather would.

Besides, her life was here. His was in Chicago. End of story.

Pushing through the gate, J.C.'s spirits took another nose dive. His plastic grocery bags had been ripped apart, the package of deli ham meant to provide lunches for the next week decimated.

And it didn't take a detective to figure out what had happened.

While the feral cats he'd chased off had been scavenging behind the house, their friends had had a picnic on his lunch meat.

As he bent to salvage what he could, he took one last look at the lighted upstairs window in the back of The Devon Rose. A silhouette moved past the closed shade, and J.C. was struck by the symbolism. Heather was there, in the shadows. Close, but out of reach.

Just like the redemption and forgiveness he yearned for.

He was working hard to find the latter. And in time, with prayer, he trusted he would succeed.

In terms of connecting with Heather, however, he was far less optimistic.

But it shouldn't matter, he reminded himself, tossing a frozen dinner into one of the bags as he stood. He hadn't come to Nantucket for romance.

He should just accept that the attractive tearoom owner was off-limits and do his best to put her out of his mind.

Except that wasn't going to be easy when he could see her lighted window every night from the doorway of his cottage.

Chapter Four

A ray of sun teased Heather awake, and with a contented sigh she turned on her side and bunched her pillow under her head. No way was she getting up yet. Monday was her day to sleep late and lounge around. And after the past busy week, she deserved a few hours of leisure.

At least there'd been no unexpected customers this Saturday or Sunday, as there had been last weekend. In fact, she hadn't had even a glimpse of Justin—J.C., she reminded herself—since the cat incident his second day on the island.

Edith kept her informed of his activities, however. So Heather was aware he'd rented a bike. Aware he'd been using his off-hours to explore the island. Aware he'd begun attending church with the Shaws.

But most of all, she was simply aware. Of him.

And that scared her.

Flopping onto her back, she turned her head to observe the new green leaves of her prized October Glory maple tree as they fluttered against a cloudless deep-blue sky. A gentle breeze wafted through her open window, and she inhaled the fresh, salty scent of the Nantucket morning, trying to relax.

That wasn't going to happen today, however, she acknowledged. Thanks to the arrival of a certain Chicago cop who'd managed to disrupt her peace of mind.

With an irritated huff, Heather threw back the covers and padded over to push the lace curtain aside and lower the sash against the slight morning chill. Most of the little guest cottage tucked among the hydrangea bushes at the back of Edith's property was hidden from her view, though she could catch a glimpse of the front door and roof if she tried. Which she did, despite a warning voice that told her to turn away. And to her dismay, that quick peek was enough to quicken her pulse.

Not good.

How in the world could she be so attracted to a man she'd spoken to for less than five minutes?

Yet she couldn't deny the almost-palpable chemistry—on her side, anyway. She'd felt it in the foyer of The Devon Rose, when J.C. had taken her hand in his strong grip and looked at her with those intense dark eyes. And she'd felt it again when he'd pulled her into the shadows by the house the night of the cat invasion. A whisper away, she'd inhaled his rugged aftershave. Felt the warmth of his hand seep into her arm and radiate through her body. Sensed that with this man protecting her, she'd be safe from any threat.

Except the one he himself represented.

That was what scared her.

Because J.C. wasn't for her. The Anderson women's bad judgment about men aside, the Chicago detective was here only for the summer. Besides, she'd learned an important lesson from her mother's experience—and from the histories she'd read about the independent Nantucket women of the past who'd run the town while the men were away on long whaling trips: take control of your own destiny. Never give anyone jurisdiction over your life—materially or emotionally.

She'd forgotten that lesson with Mark. But his betrayal had been a wake-up call. She'd been fooled once, and the shame was on him. The next time around, the shame would be hers.

Letting the delicate lace curtain fall back into place, Heather turned away from the window. Considering she hadn't seen him once in the past eight days, avoiding J.C. shouldn't be a problem, she assured herself.

And as the old saying went, out of sight, out of mind.

She hoped.

* * *

Propped against a large piece of driftwood on Ladies Beach, J.C. adjusted his baseball cap, settled his sunglasses into a more comfortable position on his nose and flipped the tab on his soda can.

This was why he'd come to Nantucket.

Not a soul was visible in either direction down the long expanse of golden sand. Edith's recommendation for a getaway spot had been perfect. At the end of a dirt road not traveled by most tourists, this secluded stretch was, as she'd promised, a quiet refuge among the busy South Shore beaches.

Tucked in at the base of a sheltered dune, his bike propped beside him, J.C. had a panoramic view of the glistening sea. It was the perfect place to spend the afternoon of his first full day off since starting work, and he intended to make the most of it.

A boat appeared in the distance, and he watched its steady progress as it followed a course parallel to the beach. Although it was rocked by swells, it rode them out without faltering or deviating from its route, secure in its ability to hold fast to its destination despite choppy seas.

That was how he wanted to be. Steadfast, confident, unshakable even in rough water. Until the shooting, he'd thought he *was* that way. He'd seen plenty of bad stuff in his thirteen years on the force. Some of it had kept him awake at night. Some of it had given him nightmares. But he'd always managed to move on. Until last month.

Because this time, the responsibility for two innocent deaths rested on his shoulders.

Not everyone agreed with that conclusion, he conceded. The internal review panel had absolved him of fault. Dennis and Ben hadn't blamed him. Nor had the families of the two men who'd lost their lives. Burke didn't, either. Everyone knew undercover work was dangerous. You accepted the risks, or you didn't volunteer.

But risks were different than mistakes. And it had to have been a mistake that had aroused his contacts' suspicions. There was no other way to explain the setup he, Jack and Scott had walked into in that cold, empty warehouse.

For the thousandth time, J.C. reviewed the facts.

Surveillance had been in place, cover officers had been in position and he'd been wired and armed. Documented identities had been provided for Jack and Scott under the assumption that the drug kingpins would do background checks on their new customers, and the men had been prepared to play their parts.

The only thing unusual about the situation had been the size of the deal, which involved the first deep-pockets customers he'd solicited for the ring. It had been big enough to persuade the leader himself to handle the transaction. Meaning it had shaped up to be exactly the kind of deal J.C. had been assigned to arrange. Catching the main man in an incriminating position would be the payoff for his nine miserable months undercover.

Bottom line, the department had expected to take down one of the most powerful narcotics rings in the city.

Then everything had fallen apart.

And two of his buddies had died.

Moisture gathered in his eyes, obscuring his vision of the sea, and he lifted an arm to wipe it away with the sleeve of his T-shirt.

Those bullets had been meant for him, too.

Once more, the two questions that continued to haunt him echoed in his mind.

Why had he been allowed to live, while other good men had died?

What had gone wrong?

As he lost sight of the boat, J.C. picked up his Bible. He wouldn't find an answer to the second question in the Good Book. But perhaps it would shed some light on the first one.

Heather opened the trunk of her car, grabbed a beach chair and her suspense novel, and headed toward the sand. Although an occasional visitor did discover her secret hideaway, Ladies Beach wasn't on most of the tourist maps—and she hoped it never would be. It was her favorite place to come on Monday afternoons in the summer. And today, with no other cars in sight, she should have the place to herself.

But as she kicked her flip-flops onto the warm sand and bent to pick them up, she spotted a lone figure in the distance. A man sitting against a piece of driftwood, reading a book.

A wave of disappointment washed over her. So much for solitude.

But it was a big beach, she consoled herself. She'd head the other way and find her own place in the sun.

She started to turn away from the interloper, but a movement caught her attention. When she cast a glance over her shoulder, he waved.

Squinting, Heather tried to identify him. But with a baseball cap covering his hair and reflective sunglasses masking his eyes, she didn't have a clue who he was.

Then he solved the mystery by removing both.

It was J.C.

And there was only one way to explain his presence, she concluded, clamping her lips together.

Edith.

The Lighthouse Lane matchmaker was at it again.

Heather held on to her temper—with an effort. But Ms. Busybody was going to get an earful later!

Taking her time, she strolled toward J.C., trying to decide on a plan of action. But when he rose— a lithe movement that revealed long, muscular legs beneath black swimming trunks and impressive biceps bulging below the sleeves of a chest-hugging T-shirt—it was all she could do to put one foot in front of the other.

The man was a hunk, pure and simple.

Funny. Usually, Heather wasn't impressed by muscles and testosterone. Why J.C. was an exception, she had no idea. But alerts were sounding in her brain, reminding her to protect her heart.

Stopping a few feet away, Heather slipped on her sunglasses, which allowed her to give him a discreet perusal. She noticed the logo on his T-shirt—for a team called the Titan Tigers—but it was the broad chest underneath that fascinated her more.

Until he reached down to set his can of soda on the sand and his sleeve pulled up to reveal the tail end of a scar that appeared to be fairly new.

Straightening, he gave her that roguish, adrenaline-producing half smile as he put his own sunglasses back on. "I thought it was you. But the outfit threw me for a minute." He gave her a swift scan. "Quite a switch from pearls and silk."

Heather shifted in the sand, regretting her choice of faded denim shorts that revealed a tad too much leg and a T-shirt that had shrunk too much from frequent washing.

She tugged at the hem and switched subjects. "Interesting logo." She gestured toward his shirt.

He looked down, as if he'd forgotten what he'd put on that morning. "Oh, yeah, it is. The Titans are a primary-school softball team I coach at my church. Small but mighty, according to their motto, though their win record might dispute that. But they have a lot of fun, and that's what counts."

His grin turned her insides to mush. As did his philosophy. A lot of kids' coaches lost sight of the fact that there were more important things than winning. "So…how did you find this out-of-the-way spot?"

"Edith recommended it when I asked about a secluded place to spend some time with a good book."

Yep, a talk with her neighbor was high on her agenda for later in the day. "What are you reading?"

He gestured to his feet, where a book bearing the name *The Holy Bible* rested on a towel next to the remnants of a sandwich.

Heather did a double take.

"You seem surprised," he remarked.

"A little."

"Why?"

She was struck by his tone. Rather than defensive or embarrassed, as she half expected it to be, it was mild—and more curious than self-conscious.

"You don't strike me as the Bible-toting type."

"Is there such a thing?"

His relaxed question threw her. The truth was, she'd always thought of Bible readers as holier-than-thou and a bit nerdy. Yet none of the people of faith she knew fit that stereotype, she acknowledged. This man was certainly far removed from that image.

"I guess not. I just assumed you'd prefer action stories in your reading, given your background."

A subtle tautness sharpened his features. "I have enough action in real life. Besides, the Bible isn't dull reading. And it offers great guidance."

"I'll have to take your word for that. When it

comes to dealing with life, I prefer to rely on myself."

It occurred to her he might take offense at her remark, but his demeanor remained placid. "You sound like my sister."

She caught the hint of affection in his tone, and a smile tugged at her lips. "If she's independent and self-sufficient, I expect we have a lot in common."

"That pretty much describes Marci."

"I have a feeling I'd like her." She took a step back. "Well…I'll let you get back to your reading. And your lunch."

"I finished lunch. I'm moving on to dessert." He snagged a bag from the towel and withdrew a smaller sack. Holding it out to her, he smiled. "Would you like to share? Edith tells me these are great."

Leaning forward, she peeked into the bag and narrowed her eyes. "Are those almond macaroons from Bartlett's Farm?"

"Yes. Edith suggested I pick up lunch there, and she said these were fantastic."

They were also one of her favorite treats. As Edith well knew, Heather thought darkly.

Capitulating, she reached into the bag and took one. She was going to have *lots* to talk about with her neighbor when she got home. "Thanks. These happen to be a particular favorite of mine."

"They can't beat the stuff you serve at your teas. Those were some of the best desserts I've ever had."

Warmth flooded her cheeks, and she backed up

a few more steps. "Thanks. I think I'll head down that way." She motioned vaguely to the west. "Enjoy your reading."

"You, too."

Swiveling around, Heather trekked down the sand in search of her own secluded spot, trying not to wonder if the dark-eyed cop was watching her.

Selecting a niche in the side of a wind- and surf-carved dune, she set up her chair, wiggled into a comfortable position, stretched her feet out in front of her, and opened her book. The novel that had kept her enthralled far too late into the night for the past week would dispel any further thoughts of J.C., she assured herself.

But today, no matter how hard she tried, she couldn't focus on the heart-racing suspense between the covers of her book.

Because her heart was already racing—thanks to a certain transplanted Chicago cop who'd staked out a spot on her private territory that was way too close for comfort.

"Is Edith here, Chester?" Heather pushed through the gate into her neighbor's backyard, passing under the rose-covered arched arbor.

Chester paused from tinkering with the lawn mower and waved a wrench toward the house. "Inside."

"Thanks."

Marching toward the back porch, she mounted the steps and called through the open door. "Edith?"

"In the dining room, dear. Come right in. And help yourself to a muffin."

Heather pulled open the screen door, ignored the fresh-baked treat on the counter in the homey kitchen—an appeasement offering…or Edith's standard prelude to a good gab session? Heather wondered—and strode into the dining room.

Her neighbor sent her a rueful grimace from her seat at the table. "I don't know how I got roped into assembling the buzz book for the Women's Club at church." She gestured to the stacks of paper in front of her. Selecting a sheet from each pile, she tapped them into a stack and positioned the long-armed stapler. "You didn't take a muffin."

Folding her arms across her chest, Heather sent Edith a pointed look. "I already had an almond macaroon from Bartlett's Farm."

Heather caught the flash of smug satisfaction on Edith's face.

"Did you go there today?"

Planting both palms flat on the table, Heather leaned closer. "Don't play innocent with me, Edith Shaw. J.C. told me you sent him to Ladies Beach."

With a determined push on the stapler, Edith linked together the individual pages she'd assembled. "What can I say? The poor man asked me to recommend a quiet beach to do some reading. Can you think of a better spot?"

"You know that's my special place on Mondays." Heather straightened up and propped her hands on her hips. "I love you dearly, Edith. But back off on this. I'm not in the market."

"Too bad." Edith tapped the next set of pages into an even line. "You couldn't do any better in the looks department. And Burke has high regard for him. Said he had to overcome a lot to get where he is on the Chicago force."

Despite herself, Heather's interest was piqued. "Like what?"

"I don't know. Burke didn't offer anything else. You could always ask J.C. himself if you're interested. It wouldn't hurt to talk to the man once in a while, you being neighbors and all."

Engaging J.C. in conversation was the last thing Heather intended to do. Every encounter with him left her on edge—and yearning for things she'd told herself she didn't need.

"We're both too busy for idle chatter. Besides, our paths don't cross very often."

"That could be remedied."

Heather sighed. "Look, could you just try to restrain yourself with the matchmaking? I don't have the time or the interest. And I'm sure it will annoy J.C., too."

"Did he seem annoyed when you showed up?"

Far from it, Heather thought. But she didn't share that with Edith. "I have scones to bake. I'll talk to you later."

Heading to The Devon Rose, Heather resolved to forget about the Chicago cop who'd taken up residence next door.

Unfortunately, he'd taken up residence in her mind as well, she realized. Every time she stepped into the foyer or passed table four, an image of him flashed through her mind. Thoughts of him even invaded her kitchen. Distracted, she found herself adding baking soda instead of baking powder to the scone recipe she'd made thousands of times.

Angry at her mistake—and at herself—Heather dumped the ruined batch of dough in the trash. If she was the praying type, she'd be calling on the Lord about now, asking Him to give her something else to think about. Anything but the cop with the dark, appealing eyes and the potent magnetism.

But maybe—if she was lucky—He'd hear her silent plea anyway.

Chapter Five

Three days later, as Heather reached across the precision-trimmed row of miniature boxwoods for one of the weeds that had dared to invade her manicured garden, her cell phone began to ring.

Snagging the offending sprout from among the hot-pink begonias, she deposited it in a bucket by her side, sat back on her heels and stripped off her gardening gloves before retrieving the phone from the brick path beside her.

"The Devon Rose."

"Hi, Heather. Do you have a minute?"

At the underlying thread of tension in her sister's question, Heather's grip on the phone tightened. "Sure. Is everything okay?"

"No." Susan's voice wavered. "Brian's in trouble again."

Since her sister had separated from her philandering husband several months ago, Heather knew thirteen-year-old Brian had been getting into minor scrapes. This one sounded major.

"What happened?"

"He and some of the kids he's been hanging around with spray painted a vulgar message on a garage door. A neighbor spotted them and called the police."

"Did the owners press charges?"

"Not after the parents chipped in to pay for the damage. But now I'm really worried about leaving Brian at home alone all summer. When I decided to get a job after Peter and I split, I felt comfortable about him being on his own. He's always been a responsible, levelheaded kid. But last week, I found a squashed beer can by the picnic table in back. Brian says he didn't drink anything, but his buddies obviously did. I just don't trust him at this point."

"What does Peter think?"

"To quote him, 'Boys will be boys.'"

"Why am I not surprised?" Disgust laced Heather's reply. She'd never thought much of Susan's husband. Even less after he began cheating on his wife.

"Here's the thing, Heather. I need to get him away from his so-called friends before he finds himself in real trouble. I know this is a huge imposition, but…could I send him to Nantucket for three weeks? I wouldn't ask if I wasn't desperate."

The shakiness in her sister's voice told Heather that Susan wasn't exaggerating her worry. But the notion of taking in a nephew she hadn't seen since her mother's funeral two years ago—one with delinquent tendencies, no less—freaked her out.

"Why don't you just ask his grandfather to keep an eye on him while you're at work?"

Heather wasn't surprised when her suggestion was greeted with shocked silence. If she hadn't been desperate herself to find an alternate solution to Susan's dilemma, she would never have mentioned their father. Talking about him had been off-limits ever since the divorce that had ripped her family apart two decades ago. Heather had never understood why Susan had kept in touch with the man who had destroyed their family, and Susan had never understood how Heather could shut out the father she'd once idolized. To protect their own relationship, they'd agreed to table any discussion about him.

"You mentioned Dad." Susan sounded stunned.

"Sorry about that." Heather took a long, slow breath, hoping the quiet of her garden would soothe her as it usually did. But today the perfect little world of tranquility and beauty she'd created didn't have its typical calming effect. Instead, she had a feeling that her predictable, orderly life was about to change. "It's just that I don't have a clue how to deal with a thirteen-year-old boy."

"You can't do any worse than I have." Her sister sniffled. "And I did think about asking Dad to teen-sit this summer, but he hasn't been feeling well lately."

It was on the tip of her tongue to ask what was wrong with him, but Heather bit back the question. She didn't want to discuss their father. He'd been out of her life for twenty years. Why should she care if he had health problems?

Reaching out, Heather plucked a tiny, insidious weed from from among the begonias. She liked nurturing the plants in her garden. Liked watching them flourish and grow under her care. And she'd learned a lot through the years. Including the fact that sometimes a plant needed to be moved to a different location in order to thrive.

She had a feeling the same might be true for Brian.

"Heather?"

Closing her eyes, Heather made the only choice her conscience would allow. "Okay, Susan. I'll give it a shot."

Her sister's effusive gratitude was heartwarming, but as Susan ended the call with a promise to get back in touch as soon as she had all the travel details hammered out, panic began to gnaw at the edges of Heather's composure. She was getting in over her head, and she knew it. But how could she turn down her sister, who was doing her best to adjust to a separation, settle into a new job and deal with a troubled teen?

At the same time, how in the world was she going to cope with a rebellious thirteen-year-old boy, who would no doubt be making this trip against his will?

As Heather gathered up her gardening tools, she

caught a glimpse of the roof of the guest cottage in Edith's backyard. And was suddenly reminded of the silent prayer she'd offered three days ago, asking God to give her something to think about besides the handsome cop.

She'd made a few other such prayers over the years. None had ever been answered, leaving her to conclude that the Almighty wasn't on her wavelength.

Too bad He'd chosen now to tune her in, she thought with a sigh.

Forty-eight hours later, seated at a table in the noisy high-school gym, Heather was still having serious misgivings about agreeing to take her nephew. And after tossing and turning for the past two nights, she was in no mood to spend the next few hours answering stupid trivia questions, even if it was a fund-raiser for a student who needed a bone marrow transplant.

On the bright side, though, maybe the game would distract her.

Grabbing a handful of popcorn from the tub in the center of the table, she popped several kernels in her mouth, did a quick survey of the gym—and almost choked when she saw a familiar jeans-clad figure standing in the doorway.

What on earth was J.C. doing here?

Coughing, she reached for a glass of water.

"Are you all right?" Red-haired Kate MacDonald, sitting beside her, touched her shoulder in concern.

Instead of answering, Heather took another swallow of water, gulped in some air and glared at Edith across the table. The men had gone to get some soft drinks and more substantial snacks, leaving Kate, Edith, Julie and Heather spaced around the table for eight.

"Edith…" Somehow Heather managed to choke out the accusatory word.

The woman gave her a blank look. "What?"

Heather tipped her head toward the door, and all three women turned.

"My goodness!" Delight suffused Edith's face, and she started to rise.

"Edith!" This time Heather said her name with more force. After one look at her, the older woman sat back down. "What's going on? This event has been sold out for weeks."

"I have no idea."

Julie squirmed in her chair, and Heather transferred her attention to the dark-haired woman. "Julie? What do you know about this?"

A flush tinted her assistant's cheeks bright pink. "Rose in Dispatch canceled yesterday. Todd invited J.C. to take her place."

Shock rippled through Heather. "You mean he's sitting *here*? At *this* table?"

"Yes."

"We worked together all afternoon, and you didn't tell me?"

"I didn't think you'd show up if you knew."

"She wouldn't have, either," Edith chimed in.

"Do I detect a bit of matchmaking here?" Kate gave the trio an amused scan.

"That's an understatement if I ever heard one," Heather muttered, trying to come up with an escape plan.

Chuckling, Kate gave her arm an empathetic pat while casting an affectionate smile at Edith. "I've been there. But, hey, it worked for me."

"Don't encourage her," Heather warned. "She already…"

"Hi, ladies. I think this is my table."

At the mellow baritone voice behind Heather, three pairs of eyes switched focus, while she kept her gaze fixed on the tub of popcorn. She'd expected to spend the next few hours sitting next to a middle-aged widow, not a handsome cop. The change in plans did not bode well for her peace of mind, which was already shaky.

"Well, sit right down and make yourself at home." Edith gestured toward the chair beside Heather's. "The men will be back in a minute. They went to the concession stand."

Pulling out the chair, J.C. settled in. A faint whiff of rugged aftershave wafted her way, and Heather squeezed the napkin in her hand into a tight ball as her heart skipped a beat. This was weird. Even Mark had never had this kind of effect on her. And J.C. wasn't even trying.

Now there was a scary thought!

"You know everyone here, don't you, J.C.?" Edith asked, every inch the proper hostess.

"Yes. Julie served me my first tea, Kate gives me a great weather report whenever we meet, and Heather—" he directed one of those pulse-disrupting, half-hitch smiles her way "—taught me a few things about cats."

"Cats?" Julie gave her employer a puzzled look. "I didn't know you were into cats."

"It's a long story." Heather was saved from further explanation by the return of the men.

Todd set a pitcher in front of J.C., and the dark-haired cop picked it up. "Would you like some soda, Heather?"

Grasping her plastic cup, she edged it toward the pitcher. "Thanks."

Once her cup was full, J.C. reached past her to fill Craig's, his sun-browned hand brushing hers. She jerked back as if she'd been burned, watching in horror as the soda in her cup sloshed out and headed toward her across the table.

Acting on instinct, she scooted her chair back— and collided with the man passing behind her, who was juggling a large tub of popcorn and a pitcher of lemonade. The popcorn rained down on her like a sudden summer shower.

Mortified, Heather closed her eyes, wishing she could melt into the floor like the wicked witch in *The Wizard of Oz*. How much worse could this night get?

A giggle erupted to her right. Kate. Another

followed on the left. Julie. She identified the deeper chuckle across the table as Chester's.

Forcing herself to open her eyes, she risked a peek at the man beside her. The suspicious twitch at the corners of his lips told her he was struggling to contain his own laughter, and heat radiated across her cheeks.

All she could do was try to make the best of an embarrassing situation, Heather decided, accepting that she'd never live this down. Pasting on a smile, she gave a vigorous shake of her head, sending kernels flying in all directions. "Popcorn, anyone?"

J.C. released the chuckle he'd been holding back and plucked a kernel from her hair. "Interesting serving method. But I don't think it would go over at your teas."

She liked the way the skin crinkled at the corners of his eyes when he smiled, Heather thought, giving him a good look for the first time. And at this proximity, she couldn't help noticing the faint glint of gold in his dark irises. His strong, clean-shaven jaw also fascinated her. A faint shadow suggested he had a heavy beard. Would his skin feel smooth or textured against the tips of her fingers? she wondered.

Startled by a sudden urge to find the answer to that question, she shifted abruptly away from him, sifting through her hair with her fingers to remove the remaining popcorn. The subtle change in his eyes gave her the uncomfortable feeling he might have sensed her impulse—but that was impossible. The man might be a detective, but he wasn't a mind reader.

When she discovered Edith watching her from across the table, however, Heather had a sinking feeling her neighbor *had* guessed her thoughts.

Meaning that while she'd unjustly accused Edith of setting her up tonight, there was a very good possibility the Lighthouse Lane matchmaker would be hard at work again in the not-too-distant future.

"David Niven, Cary Grant and Loretta Young."

Every head at the table swiveled toward him as J.C. responded to the emcee's question in the old movies category.

"How do you know that?" Heather gave him a skeptical look.

"I like vintage films."

"I've never heard of *The Bishop's Wife*."

"It's a classic Christmas movie. You should rent it sometime."

"Unless one of you knows more than J.C. on this one, I'm going with his answer," Edith declared, surveying the table. When no one responded, she jotted down the names of the three stars.

As J.C. reached out to pick up his cup of soda, Heather shifted slightly away from him. She'd been doing that all night, every time he got a little too close, sending a clear message.

Keep your distance.

It wasn't because she found him unappealing, J.C. had concluded. Her hazel eyes told him she felt the electricity between them as much as he did. She just didn't want any part of it. The question was why? While his temporary stay on the island might account for some of her caution, he sensed her skittishness had a far deeper source.

And the detective in him wanted to solve that mystery.

As did the man.

That was one of the reasons he'd agreed to attend tonight. If Todd hadn't told him Heather would be at the table, he'd have opted for a good book or a video in the quiet of his cottage. But he hadn't been able to pass up the opportunity to share his evening with the lovely tearoom owner. Even if she was currently giving him the cold shoulder.

"You should know that one, Heather."

At Julie's comment, Heather gave the woman a blank look. "Sorry." She cleared her throat. "I missed the question."

"What's the official name of the park where the Arch in St. Louis is located?" Kate repeated.

"The Jefferson National Expansion Memorial."

"Woo-hoo! We are going to win this sucker!" Edith chortled, jotting down the final answer of the night.

"How come Julie said you'd know that?" J.C. directed his question to Heather as the game sheets were collected and the tabulations began.

"I lived there years ago."

He lifted an eyebrow. "I had the impression you were a Nantucket native."

"I feel like one. My mom and I moved here twenty years ago, when I was fourteen. She'd inherited the house from her aunt."

"Just the two of you?"

"Yes. She started The Devon Rose, and we ran it together until…until she died of pancreatic cancer two years ago."

He leaned closer to hear her suddenly subdued voice. Close enough for the faint caress of her breath on his cheek to quicken his pulse. "I'm sorry. I hear that's a rough way to go."

She eased back and blinked several times. "It was."

"What happened to your dad?"

Anger displaced the grief in her eyes, and her tone grew bitter. "I have no idea. He and my mother split right before we moved here. I haven't talked to him in twenty years."

J.C. nodded in empathy. He knew all about estrangements—and the emotional toll they could take. "Family rifts are hard."

Her features grew taut. "He cheated on my mother. And I don't have any respect for people who break their vows or refuse to honor their commitments."

J.C.'s gut twisted. He could relate to that, too. "Do you have any other family?"

"A sister in St. Louis, recently separated. And a

thirteen-year-old nephew." She shook her head. "Who's about to land on my doorstep. Tomorrow."

"Why do I get the feeling you're not looking forward to that?"

Heather glanced toward Edith. J.C. followed suit. The older woman was engaged in an animated conversation with the emcee, who'd strolled over to chat while the scores were tabulated. With the din in the gym, J.C. couldn't hear one word they were saying. Nor was his landlady paying any attention to her tablemates.

Dropping her voice, Heather kept one eye on the older woman as she responded. "I'm not. He's been getting into some trouble, and my sister thought a change of scene might help."

"What kind of trouble?"

"The latest problems are possible underage drinking and vandalism." Heather tucked her hair behind her ear and shook her head. "I have no idea what I'm going to do with him. My experience with boys that age would fit in this—" she tapped her empty plastic cup against the table in agitation "—with room to spare."

Not good, J.C. reflected. While he admired Heather for her willingness to help her sister out, she was setting herself up for a rough ride. Thirteen-year-old boys could get into a mess of trouble. He'd witnessed plenty of it on the street—and in his own life, thanks to Nathan.

For a brief instant, he entertained the notion of

offering her help if things got dicey. But he didn't have much experience with kids that age, either. The ten- and eleven-year-old Titan Tigers were young enough to be relatively innocent. And he hadn't done a very good job with Nathan when his brother had been a rebellious teen.

Besides, he didn't need the complication. He'd come here to get away from problems. The last thing he wanted to do was deal with a teen delinquent. He had too much on his plate already.

"Okay, listen up, everyone. We have our winners!"

The booming announcement from the emcee saved him from having to respond, and he was grateful for the reprieve as he directed his attention toward the front of the gym.

When the grand prize–winning team was announced, Edith clapped Todd on the back and threw her arms around a blushing Chester. "I told you we'd win!"

A basket filled with prizes was delivered to their table, and while Edith dived in, J.C. grinned at Heather. "It's refreshing to see such enthusiasm."

"She does get carried away." Heather gave the woman a wry look.

"J.C., come over here and take first pick of these prizes," Edith called over to him. "We wouldn't have won without you. You answered more than half the questions."

"That's okay. You all divide everything up. I was just a last-minute sub."

"Nonsense. You can't leave empty-handed. Do you want me to pick something out for you?"

"Sure."

Pushing aside a box of gourmet chocolate-covered cranberries, Edith pulled out an array of envelopes containing gift cards and riffled through them. Selecting one, she handed it to him. "You'll enjoy this."

He took it, noting The Summer House name and a 'Sconset return address.

"That restaurant has the most divine terrace overlooking the ocean—and the food is great," Edith told him. "Very romantic. And that should more than cover a dinner for two." She sent a meaningful glance toward the woman on his right.

J.C. caught the dark look Heather shot the older woman as he removed the plastic gift card from the envelope and tucked it in his wallet. No surprise there. Given the clear No Trespassing signals Heather had been sending him all night, he would have expected her to resist any matchmaking efforts. But it was nice to know he had an ally in Edith.

"Are you ready to go, Chester?" Heather rose. "I want to get an early start on my baking tomorrow."

"Sure thing." He stood, and Edith picked up her purse.

"How did you get here?" Edith asked J.C.

"I walked. It's a beautiful evening."

"But the return trip will be a bit of a hike at this hour. Why don't you ride back with us?"

In his peripheral vision, he saw Heather stiffen—and took that as his cue. "Thanks, Edith. But I could use the exercise after sitting all evening."

Heather's relief was almost palpable. She gave him a polite, if reserved, goodbye, all the while keeping her distance, and walked out of the gym without a backward look.

Stymied, J.C. planted his fists on his hips and watched her depart.

"Did she give you the brush-off?" Todd moved beside him and grinned as Julie conversed with Kate and Craig.

"That would be a polite way to put it."

"Don't take it personally. She's like that with all eligible men. I think it goes back to a bad experience she had with some guy she was dating a few years ago. Caught him in a compromising position, as I recall. Julie knows more about that than I do. But trust me, you're not being singled out for special attention."

Julie reclaimed Todd, and J.C. walked out with them, breaking off with a wave once they stepped outside.

As he strode down the dark street toward Lighthouse Lane, he thought about Todd's comment. He supposed her bad dating experience might explain Heather's skittishness around him.

Yet he sensed there was more to it.

Had any other woman sent such strong back-off signals, J.C. knew he would have lost interest by now. But Heather's brush-off—and the reasons behind it—intrigued him. He liked a good challenge, had always been fascinated by puzzles. That was one of the reasons he'd been drawn to detective work.

And Miss Jefferson National Expansion Memorial was one big puzzle just waiting to be solved.

Chapter Six

It was going to be worse than she'd thought.

As Heather spotted her nephew among the arriving passengers the next day at the airport, her stomach dropped. His hair was the same striking shade of sun-ripened wheat she remembered. And he still had the amazing blue eyes they'd all marveled at when he was a toddler.

But everything else had changed.

The eager, innocent little boy who'd had such fun chasing sand crabs during family visits had disappeared. In his place was a tall, gangly adolescent wearing sloppy, oversize clothes and a defiant scowl that screamed, "I don't want to be here, and someone's gonna pay!"

Namely, her.

Trying not to panic, she forced her stiff lips into a smile, lifted a hand and waved.

Their gazes connected. Held for a moment. But

he didn't return her greeting or her smile. Instead, he slowed his pace, shifted his backpack into a different position and ignored her as he approached.

Her stomach clenched. Every instinct in her body told her to turn around and run. Far and fast. But common sense held her in place. She'd agreed to take him in. She couldn't give up before they'd even said hello.

"Hi, Brian." As he shuffled to a stop in front of her, she realized they were at eye level. "Wow. You've really gotten tall."

"Isn't that what growing up is all about?"

Sarcasm dripped off his words, and a chill ran through her. Susan had said he'd developed an attitude, but Heather had hoped it wouldn't carry over to Nantucket.

No such luck. He'd obviously put her in the enemy camp, beside his mother.

"Well, let's get your luggage and head home. Are you hungry?"

"I had a burger in the airport in Boston."

"How about a piece of chocolate cake, then? I baked the one you liked so much when you were here last time." She kept her smile pasted in place and managed to maintain an upbeat tone.

"I don't eat much sweet stuff anymore. Do you have any chips?"

"No. But we can get some."

"Whatever."

Although Heather tried her best to draw him out

during the short drive back to the house, her efforts produced no more than monosyllabic responses. The guest room she'd readied for him was met with nothing more than a cursory sweep as he dropped his backpack onto the floor, sat on the edge of the bed and withdrew a laptop from a side compartment of his suitcase.

Heather watched as he booted up, her panic accelerating. She hadn't expected Brian to be happy about the trip. But neither had she expected him to be rude, disrespectful and obnoxious.

All at once he uttered a word that made her blink. The kind of word that had been forbidden when she was growing up.

"Brian."

He ignored her.

She tried again. "Brian…I don't tolerate that kind of language in this house. And I'm sure your mother doesn't allow it at home, either."

Bent over his computer, he scowled and shoved his too-long bangs aside. "It's not working."

"What's not working?"

"The Internet."

"You're not plugged in."

"To what?"

"The modem."

He gaped at her. "You don't have Wi-Fi?"

"No."

He uttered the word again.

"Brian…" Heather tried to hold on to her temper. "I said we don't use that word in this house."

He smirked at her. "So what are you going to do? Send me home?"

Checkmate, she thought grimly. He'd like nothing better than to be sent back to the friends Susan wanted to purge from his life.

Turning on her heel, she headed for the door.

"Hey…how am I going to check my e-mail?"

"According to your mother, you're not supposed to have any contact with anyone at home except her." She spoke over her shoulder as she walked.

He said the word again. Three times, in rapid succession. Then he slammed the cover down on his computer. "That stinks! This whole trip stinks."

"Yeah. I already got that message." She paused on the threshold. "But we're stuck with each other for the next three weeks. You can have some fun…or you can sulk. It's your choice. I'll see you at breakfast."

Easing the door shut behind her, Heather closed her eyes and drew a shaky breath. Three more weeks of this.

Brian was right.

It stunk.

The gate to Heather's garden was open.

Frowning, J.C. applied the hand brakes on his bike as he approached the entrance to her side yard. Edith had told him about the care Heather lavished on her garden, how she regarded it as a private sanctuary. He'd never seen the gate open.

As he tightened his grip on the brakes, he realized the gate was listing slightly on its hinges. In the distance, he spotted Heather walking toward him down the brick path, juggling a variety of tools.

And she didn't look happy.

Coming to a full stop, he straddled the bike, balancing it as she approached. Her step faltered when she caught sight of him, but then she picked up her pace again.

"Problem with the gate?"

She stopped just inside the opening to deposit her tools on the ground. Since their last encounter at the trivia fund-raiser three days ago, faint shadows had appeared under her eyes. The kind produced by worry and sleeplessness. No doubt due to her nephew's arrival, J.C. concluded.

Rubbing her palms on her jeans, she surveyed the gate with disgust. "Yeah. It didn't appreciate being kicked."

Not liking the sound of that, J.C. got off the bike. "Who kicked it?"

"My nephew." Distress flared in her eyes, and she folded her arms tight across her chest. "I caught him heading out this way a little while ago, and he wasn't happy about being told to stay on the premises unless he's with an adult."

"Where is he now?"

"Where he's been since he arrived. Up in his

room. Listening to music on his iPod or playing computer games on his laptop. He only comes out to eat—generally when I'm not around."

"Sounds like it's been a rough beginning."

"Yeah."

She angled away from him on the pretext of sorting through her tools, but he caught the suspicious sheen in her eyes. And it shook him. He'd pegged Heather as a woman who always maintained control. If the situation with her nephew had rattled her this much, it must be a lot worse than he'd thought.

J.C. didn't want to get involved in a messy family dispute. The Lord knew he'd botched enough of those with his own siblings. But he couldn't walk away, either. When a person was in distress, there was only one option. You went to their aid. It was how he operated on the job—and off.

Resigned, he set the bike's kickstand and joined her. "Let me take a look."

He half expected her to balk, but to his surprise she backed off instead.

Bending down, he examined the damage, giving her a chance to pull herself together. There was a bit of rot in the weathered wood around the hinge, he noted. But still…the kid must be pretty strong to have jimmied the nail loose with a kick or two. And people who lashed out in anger made him uneasy. No matter their age.

"Do you have a hammer there?" He gestured toward the tools.

"Yes. But I can fix this. You don't need to bother."

She sounded more composed now, though he still detected a hint of shakiness in her words.

"I'm down here already. Besides, it's a two-person job." He adjusted the gate. "If you can hold this in place. I'll drive the nail back in."

She complied without further argument, and several strong whacks with the hammer corrected the problem.

Rising, J.C. indicated the hinge. "There's some rot down there. You're going to need to replace that board pretty soon."

"Okay. Thanks."

She held out her hand for the hammer.

He handed it over.

This was his chance to leave. To walk away from her problems.

But he couldn't move. Her obvious worry and stress held him in place—as did a compelling need to relieve them. "So does your nephew intend to spend the entire three weeks in his room?"

Her shoulders drooped a fraction. "It would appear that way. I tried to get him to go to the beach with me yesterday, but he had no interest. I call him for meals, but he doesn't show up. He prefers to forage in the kitchen when I'm not around."

"What does his mother say?"

Heather shoved her hands in the pockets of her jeans and toed a stray leaf off the path. "I haven't given her all the details. She's dealing with a lot of stuff right now, and I'd rather try to make this work before raising alarm bells."

"So what's your plan?"

She lifted her head, her expression bleak. "I wish I had one. I don't know a thing about thirteen-year-old boys." She drew in a long, slow breath. Let it out. "I'm open to suggestions."

Surprise robbed J.C. of speech. Heather didn't strike him as the kind of woman who often admitted she was in over her head or asked for help. So her tentative appeal for assistance underscored her desperation. And he wished he could offer her some counsel. But he'd failed with his own teenage brother. Any advice he gave might make things worse instead of better.

When the silence between them lengthened, a pink tinge colored her cheeks, and she bent down to retrieve the rest of her tools. "Sorry. I didn't mean to hold you up. You probably have to get to work."

As she started to turn away, J.C. realized she'd interpreted his reticence as indifference. He couldn't let that impression go uncorrected.

Reaching out, he touched her arm, stopping her. "I'm on nights this week. I have a few minutes."

She checked him out over her shoulder. He returned her gaze steadily, and at last she turned back toward him. "I just assumed you'd run into a lot of troubled kids in your line of work. And that you might have some ideas about how I could try to connect with him."

Folding his arms across his chest, he propped a shoulder against the gate. Although she'd dropped her guard a little, she hadn't invited him into her private haven, he noted. But she wasn't edging away, either. And they were talking. That was an improvement.

"Most of the kids I see on the job have done far worse things than Brian. But a lot of them start this way. And anger is often the root cause. During adolescence, kids are testing their limits, anyway, and if they're mad at the world or feel they've been treated unfairly by life, they're apt to push those limits hard. And to get in a lot more trouble than the average teenager, moving from minor pranks to increasingly serious offenses. Your nephew may be heading down that road."

"So how do I get him on a different road? While he's here, anyway."

"You could try some tough love. Lay down the ground rules, stick to them, build in consequences if they're broken." He raked his fingers through his hair and shook his head. "But to be honest, that doesn't always work." He'd tried it with Nathan, on the advice of a school counselor. Instead of setting his brother on the right path, it had made him more resentful and rebellious. The same could happen with Brian.

"That's kind of hard to do when you're not even a parent."

"Yeah, I know."

She tilted her head and studied him. "You sound as if you're speaking from experience."

J.C. swallowed past the sudden tightness in his throat. He didn't talk much about his background. It was too painful. But if it helped Heather get through these next three weeks…

Shoving his hands into his pockets, he balled them into fists. "I am. I was responsible for my brother and sister from the time I was eighteen and they were fifteen and thirteen. And I didn't do the best job of raising them."

A flicker of empathy softened her features. "What happened to your parents?"

"My father disappeared when I was sixteen. No one missed him." He did his best to keep the bitterness out of his voice, but some crept in despite his efforts. "Two years later, my mother was hit by a car. I got to the E.R. before she died, in time to promise her I'd take care of my siblings."

"That's a lot of responsibility to put on an eighteen-year-old."

He shrugged. "There wasn't anyone else. And I didn't mind. For me, family always came first. But good intentions don't always lead to good results. Marci's okay now, but Nathan…" He shook his head. "He has a long way to go. That's why I may not be the best person to advise you on Brian."

"But you were only a teenager yourself when you took on the care of your family, J.C. Not much older than your brother. And I'm assuming you became the breadwinner, too. While going to college?"

"Yeah." Her gentle words, and the tender compassion in her eyes, were playing havoc with his self-control. In all these years, no one except Marci had ever bothered to think about the toll that being a full-time student, a full-time employee and a full-time parent had exacted on him. Not that he'd ever expected any accolades for doing what had to be done. But it was nice to have his efforts acknowledged. Especially by this woman.

For the first time since they'd met, Heather reached out to him instead of drawing away, briefly touching his arm with her slender fingers. He could feel their warmth through the cotton of his shirt—and it radiated to his heart. As did the admiration in her eyes.

"I have a feeling you did the best you could with limited tools, J.C. And I also suspect you've learned a lot through the years. So I appreciate your help."

As the spot where her hand had connected with his arm began to cool, he tried to regain his balance. He'd planned to offer Heather a few thoughts, then step away from her messy situation. And he could still do that.

Couldn't he?

One look into her tender eyes gave him his answer.

Resigned, he withdrew a grocery receipt and a pen from his pocket and scribbled down some numbers. "I'll tell you what. If anything comes up with Brian and you'd like to talk about it, call my cell—anytime." He held out the slip of paper.

She inspected the flimsy sheet as a few heartbeats of silence passed. Then she reached out and took it. "Thank you."

"And keep remembering he's only here for three weeks."

The whisper of a smile tugged at her lips. "Why does that feel like an eternity right now?"

One corner of his mouth hitched up. "You'll get through it." He was tempted to lay his hand against the gentle sweep of her cheek in a gesture of reassurance—and caring. But there was no way he wanted to put the fragile connection they'd just established at risk. Instead, he checked his watch and eased away. "I need to get ready for work. And I'm serious about that." He gestured to the slip of paper in her hand. "Call me if I can help."

Lifting a hand in farewell, he retreated to the street for the short ride back to his cottage.

Minutes later, as he stashed his bike in Chester's garage and headed down the flagstone path toward his front door, a light came on in Heather's room. Tonight the shade was up, and as he caught a glimpse of her moving past the window, he was reminded of the night of the cat invasion, when she'd been only a shadowed silhouette, unreachable behind the closed shade.

Things had changed, thanks to the arrival of a

nephew who'd disrupted her neat, orderly world and pushed her to seek input from a man she'd gone out of her way to avoid. And J.C. had mixed feelings about that.

On one hand, he was sorry for the stress it was causing her.

But on a selfish level, he was glad it had also prompted her to dismantle a few of the barriers around her heart.

The room was a pigsty.

Heather had waited until she heard Brian's door open before heading upstairs to follow J.C.'s advice from last night and demonstrate some tough love. She hadn't wanted to risk having the teen ignore her knock. This way, he'd find her waiting in the doorway when he returned from the bathroom.

But she hadn't expected to find this...mess. The room was trashed. Literally. Trying to tamp down her anger, she scanned the candy wrappers, empty soda cans, dirty plates and glasses, crushed potato chips and the half-eaten piece of the chocolate cake he'd claimed he didn't want but that had been disappearing from the kitchen in hefty chunks since his arrival.

Her lips setting into a grim line, she folded her arms across her chest, turned her back on the room and blocked the doorway.

One minute later, the bathroom door opened. Brian took three steps down the hall. Spotted her. Stopped.

"What's going on?" He gave her a wary look.

"We need to talk."

"About what?"

She jerked a finger over her shoulder. "About that disaster area, for one thing."

He shoved his hands into the pockets of his baggy pants and glared at her. "I like it the way it is."

"I don't. And this is my house. So we're going to talk about some ground rules. First, you're going to clean up the room and keep it that way. Second, if you want to eat, you eat in the kitchen. Third, I don't like freeloaders. Starting this afternoon, you're going to help with cleanup after my tea guests leave. We'll also build in some beach time and do other fun things, if you want to. The last part's your choice. The first part isn't."

She saw the sudden stubborn jut of his jaw and braced herself. She'd expected him to balk—and she was prepared.

"What if I don't want to do any of that?"

She closed the distance between them and folded her arms across her chest. "Then I am going to shadow you twenty-four-seven."

His mouth dropped open. "What do you mean?"

"Just what I said. I'm going to stick so close to you that you won't be able to breathe without smelling my shampoo."

"You can't do that. You have to run this tea place."

"I have an assistant. And Edith will fill in for me if necessary."

His eyes narrowed, assessing her. She didn't blink—but she hoped he wouldn't call her bluff. The truth was, she *did* have to run the tearoom. While she could get Edith to help out for a day or two if Brian balked and she had to actually implement her plan, she was counting on him getting so sick of her hovering that he'd fall in line within the first twenty-four hours.

When the rigid line of his shoulders eased a fraction, she knew she'd won.

"This stinks."

"We've had that conversation before." Relief coursed through her, and she stepped aside, motioning him into the room. "Get started in here. And be downstairs at noon for lunch."

He folded his arms across his chest and didn't move.

Heather shrugged. "Start when you like. But I want this place cleaned up by the end of the day. The dust mop and vacuum are in the hall closet."

With that, she walked down the hall and descended the steps, hoping she appeared strong and in control.

But on the inside she was a quivering mass of nerves.

Because if the tough love she'd just applied didn't do the trick, she had no idea what to try next.

Eight hours later, Heather was feeling better about things. She'd heard the vacuum rev up around noon, and Brian had shown up for lunch. He hadn't deigned to talk with her as he'd wolfed down a turkey sandwich, but he'd been there. The last tea guests had departed, and he'd come when she'd called him. Julie had had to dash off for a dentist appointment, so Heather had dispatched Brian to bus the remaining tables in the twin parlors.

As she wiped off the stainless-steel prep station in the middle of the kitchen, he pushed through the swinging door, carrying a tray with a dozen teacups and saucers on it.

"You can put that here, Brian." She indicated the prep station and turned toward the sink.

Silence met her instruction, and she looked over her shoulder. As she watched, he held the tray out and very deliberately dropped it to the floor. The delicate teacups and saucers, each one of a kind from the collection she and her mother had amassed, shattered on the tile floor.

"Oops." He gave her a defiant smirk.

Shock reverberated through Heather, followed by a shaft of pain. Closing the distance between them, she dropped to one knee, picked up one of the larger shards and cradled it in her hand. It was the edge of the gilded scalloped cup given to her and her mother by one of their regular customers, an older woman who had become a close friend. Purchased for them in a tiny Cotswold antique store during a trip to England, it had been her way of saying thank-you for the many pleasant hours she'd spent at The

Devon Rose. Every cup had a story like that, which Heather often told to her patrons as she served them.

Now a dozen of them were gone.

Tears blinded her, fueled by grief and anger. Such destructive behavior was outside her realm of experience.

"Go upstairs." She choked out the words.

Silence.

"I said *go upstairs*."

"Aunt Heather, I…"

She lifted her face, and Brian stopped speaking. For the first time since his arrival, he looked uncertain. And more like the little boy she'd once caught stealing a cookie ten minutes before dinner, after his mother had told him he couldn't have one. Shamefaced. Guilty. Aware he'd stepped over the line.

But at the moment she didn't care.

"Go upstairs." Her voice shook.

After a brief hesitation, he did as she told him.

Heather didn't know how long she knelt on the floor beside the shattered porcelain that represented so many memories. But when, at last, she rose, she marched over to the phone and punched in her sister's number. She'd been afraid all along she'd find herself in over her head with the rebellious teen. And everything that had happened since he'd stepped off the plane had validated those fears. It was time to send him home. He was Susan's problem, not hers.

Her sister answered on the second ring.

"Susan…it's Heather."

"Hi. Can you hold a minute?"

Susan didn't give her sister a chance to reply. Instead, Heather was treated to some odd thumping sounds as she waited for Susan to return to the phone.

Thirty seconds later, Susan's frazzled voice came over the line. "Sorry about that. I just walked in, and I had to shut the door. You're never going to believe what happened today."

"Try me." Her sister's day couldn't have been any worse than her own, Heather thought, tension continuing to coil in her stomach.

"For starters, I got handed a huge project at work this afternoon that will require lots of overtime. Klutz that I am, I also sprained my ankle last night and am now hobbling around on crutches. And I just found out that a bunch of the kids in the group Brian was hanging around with got busted for smoking marijuana last night. I am *so* glad he's out of here for a while."

At Susan's download of information, Heather wavered. Especially after the last piece of news. Fortunately, Brian hadn't yet gotten into any serious trouble. But if he'd been in that group last night…

"So how's everything going out there?"

Heather drew a resigned breath. "It's been a little rough. But I'm coping."

"I'm sorry for putting you to all this inconvenience." There was a hint of tears in Susan's voice.

"But he really is a good kid. This separation has torn him apart, and he's taking it out on everybody. I'm hoping once he adjusts to the new reality, he'll settle down. Keeping him in line in the meantime, though, has been a challenge. Is he around?"

"He went up to his room a little while ago."

Susan sighed. "I doubt he wants to talk to me, anyway. But tell him I called, okay? And give him my love."

"Sure. Take care of yourself, Susan. Put that foot up."

"Yeah. That's what the doctor said." A disgusted sound came over the line. "I wonder if physicians know how unrealistic some of their advice is? Listen, I'll talk to you tomorrow, okay? And call me if Brian gives you any real trouble."

"Right. Take care, Susan."

As Heather gave the end button a frustrated jab, she wondered how Susan defined the term *real trouble.* In light of the marijuana news, she doubted her sister would apply that term to broken teacups.

But Heather viewed the episode differently. By her definition, when it came to real trouble, Brian was up to his neck in it.

And she didn't see how things could get any worse.

Chapter Seven

❧

The money was gone.

Puzzled, Heather inspected the kitchen counter again. She was certain she'd left the eight twenty-dollar bills she'd gotten at the ATM this morning near the telephone. But they were nowhere in sight.

She searched her purse, on the off chance she'd tucked them in there during a distracted moment today. And there had been plenty of those, thanks to Brian.

Brian.

Heather closed her eyes. She didn't want to believe her nephew had taken the money. Yet where else could it have gone?

He'd had the opportunity, too, when she'd gone to sit in her garden at twilight, hoping the peaceful ambiance would help calm her after the distressing incident with the teacups.

But after forty-five minutes, she'd given up. Even

her garden hadn't been able to soothe her. Nothing, she suspected, was going to restore order to her world except Brian's departure. And that was still two and a half weeks away.

Since coming back inside, she'd focused on the only thing she seemed to control at the present— her kitchen. She'd reorganized her tea rack. Folded linen napkins into precise squares. Shaved milk chocolate into curls to garnish the white-chocolate cheesecake squares that were on tomorrow's menu. She hadn't heard a peep out of Brian.

Now, at ten-thirty, he might be in bed. But she wouldn't sleep a wink until she addressed the missing-money situation. Although she had no idea what she was supposed to do if he denied taking it.

Hoping inspiration would strike once she confronted him, Heather ascended the stairs and headed down the hall toward his closed door. She took a deep breath, lifted her hand and rapped on the wood.

"Brian…I need to talk to you."

No response.

She wasn't surprised.

Straightening her shoulders, she rapped again. "Brian, I'm coming in. We need to talk."

Without waiting for permission, she opened the door and stepped into the room.

On a peripheral level, she was aware he'd cleaned things up. The bed had been made, the floors swept, the area rug vacuumed.

The problem was, it was too clean.

And Brian was nowhere in sight.

The bottom fell out of her stomach.

"Brian?"

Her raised voice echoed in the empty room. And reechoed in the hall, when she stepped out and tried again.

Returning to his room, she opened the closet.

His clothes had vanished.

And his suitcase and backpack were gone, too.

Her heart hammering, she ran down the steps and tried calling him again on the first floor, with the same results.

A quick tour of the yard produced nothing, either.

Doing her best to tamp down her rising panic, Heather tried to hold on to rational thought as she reached into the pocket of her jeans for her car keys, already in a search mode. Where could he be? What should she do? Who should she call?

Her fingers encountered a slip of paper, and she pulled it out. A grocery receipt. J.C.'s—from the night he'd helped her fix her gate.

Turning it over, she found his cell number scribbled on the other side.

He'd said to phone him if anything came up with Brian, she recalled. Anytime.

Although his offer had touched her, she'd never intended to take him up on it. Each encounter with him exposed her heart to too much risk.

But he *was* a cop. And cops were good in emergencies.

Perhaps he wouldn't apply that term to a runaway teen on quiet Nantucket Island.

But as far as Heather was concerned, it fit.

At the jarring ring of his cell phone, J.C. froze with his arm halfway into the sleeve of his uniform shirt. He was used to late calls in Chicago; being a detective was a 24/7 job. But since beginning his leave, there had been no reason for anyone to call him after ten.

Unless it was a family emergency.

Maybe Marci was in trouble.

Grabbing the phone, he punched the talk button. "Yes?"

"J.C.?"

It wasn't Marci.

"Heather?" He thought it was her, but the voice was so tentative and shaky, he wasn't certain.

"Yes. Listen, I'm sorry to disturb you this late. But Brian is missing."

He pushed his arm through the sleeve. "What do you mean by missing?"

"He's not in the house. His clothes are gone. And the money I got out of the ATM this morning isn't where I left it on the counter." Her voice hitched on the last word.

J.C. put the phone on speaker and set it on the dresser as he shrugged his shirt into position and rapidly buttoned it. "Okay, we'll get this figured out. Do you have any idea why he left?"

"Yes. I tried the tough-love approach this morning. It didn't go over well."

As she went on to describe what had happened—including the dropped-tray incident—the creases in J.C.'s brow deepened. The strict tactic hadn't worked with Nathan, either. You'd think he'd have learned to keep his mouth shut when it came to advice for teens, he thought in disgust.

"When did you last see him?" The question came out clipped as he slung his equipment belt around his waist and buckled it.

"I heard him upstairs at about quarter to nine, right before I went out in the garden."

"What was he wearing?" As he asked the question, J.C. pulled out his notebook.

"Last time I saw him, he had on oversize beige cargo pants, a red St. Louis Cardinals sweatshirt and sport shoes."

"What does he look like?"

"My height, wheat-colored hair, blue eyes, thin."

"Okay." He finished writing. "That's good enough for now. I'm on nights this week, and I'll head in a little early. I'll also call in his description so the officers on duty can keep an eye out for him."

"What can I do to help?"

"Stick close to home, in case he comes back or calls. A lot of times kids do."

But not always, J.C. acknowledged. Nathan had sometimes disappeared for days at a time. J.C. had lost count of the number of nights he'd spent on the street when he should have been studying, combing the neighborhood in the wee hours of the morning for his kid brother.

In general, all he'd gotten for his efforts had been a bad case of exhaustion. Nathan had learned early on how to disappear.

Brian, on the other hand, was new to this game. And there were far fewer places to hide on Nantucket than there had been in the rough Chicago neighborhood filled with dark alleys that J.C. and his siblings had called home. Besides, this was an island. He could only go so far.

Unless...

"I can't just sit around, J.C."

Heather's agitated protest interrupted his thoughts.

"I know it's hard. But give it a few hours, okay? If he doesn't show up, we'll adjust the plan."

Silence met his suggestion. Followed by a sigh of capitulation.

"Okay. But will you keep me updated?"

"Absolutely."

"I don't know what I'm going to tell Susan. She trusted me with him, and I've let her down."

J.C. knew exactly how Heather felt. He'd been there with both his siblings. And it wasn't a good place.

"This isn't your fault, Heather. You didn't ask for the responsibility, and you dealt with a bad situation in the best way you knew how. Don't blame yourself."

A couple of beats of silence passed, and when she responded, her gentle tone took him off guard. "You know, that sounds like the kind of reassurance an eighteen-year-old student I heard about yesterday could have used a long time ago. And maybe still needs to hear."

At her kindness and empathy even in the midst of her own crisis, a long-cold place in J.C.'s heart suddenly warmed, as if touched by a ray of sun peeking through the clouds on a chilly, overcast day.

"Thanks." The word came out scratchy, and he cleared his throat. "I'll talk to you soon."

Ending the call, he phoned the station with Brian's description and retrieved his bike from the garage. He didn't have to report for duty for an hour, and he had an idea he wanted to check out first. A thirteen-year-old was savvy enough to know it wouldn't be easy to vanish in a place the size of Nantucket. If he really wanted to disappear, Brian would have to find a way to leave the island. And flying wouldn't be an option. It was too expensive, and too easy to track.

That left the ferry. The last one pulled out at ten o'clock, and J.C. doubted Brian would have found his way to the dock in time to catch it, given his unfamiliarity with the town. But he might stick close to the wharf and try to catch one of the early morning boats, hoping that Heather wouldn't even have missed him by then.

Pedaling along mist-shrouded Centre Street, his

bike tires humming on the pavement, J.C. knew his theory could be off base. He'd guessed wrong plenty of times with Nathan. But if he was a thirteen-year-old kid wanting to disappear, he'd be hiding out near one of the two ferry wharfs.

The streetlights, hazy orbs in the darkness, provided more atmosphere than illumination as he approached Steamboat Wharf, deserted at this hour on a Wednesday night. Fog was beginning to roll in, giving the scene an eerie feel. He'd start here, where the car ferry docked. If he didn't have any luck, he'd check in at the station, then nose around the day ferry pier.

Propping his bike beside a shuttered souvenir stand, J.C. set off along the wharf, searching the shadows for a rebellious kid who didn't want to be found.

Just as he'd so often done in vain for his brother.

Hoping tonight he'd have better luck.

She was going stir crazy.

Pacing around the kitchen of The Devon Rose, Heather was sorry she'd agreed to wait at home on the off chance Brian might return. She'd seen his defiant expression. Felt his hostility and anger.

He wasn't coming back on his own.

And she couldn't sit around for another two hours, doing nothing.

Grabbing her keys and purse off the counter, she swung toward the door. But as she reached for the knob, the phone rang.

A surge of adrenaline shot through her, and she dashed for the phone, yanking it out of its holder.

"Yes?"

"Heather, it's J.C. I found him."

Every muscle in her body went limp, and she clutched the edge of the counter. "Is he all right?"

"Yes. He's huddled behind a Dumpster near the Hy-Line Cruises office. How do you want to handle this? He hasn't seen me."

"I'll come down. From what Susan's said, I don't think he's favorably inclined toward the police. It might be better if I'm the one who confronts him."

"Okay. I'll stick close until you get here. Why don't you park near my bike, at the entrance to Straight Wharf, and walk down? I'll watch for you."

"I'll be there in less than ten minutes."

As Heather dashed for her garage, then maneuvered her car through the great, gray, billowing waves of fog swirling through the narrow streets, she had no idea what she was going to say to Brian. Nothing she'd tried had made any impact. She doubted inspiration would strike this time when they were face-to-face.

But she could hope.

Parking beside J.C.'s bike, Heather plunged into the mist—and immediately realized she should have put on a slicker. Already dampness was seeping through the cotton of her shirt and jeans, sending a shiver rippling through her. By the time she got home, she'd be…

"Heather…"

The soft voice came from behind her, and she whirled around. "J.C.! Sorry. I must have walked right past you."

"You were moving at a pretty good clip. Brian's up ahead." He gestured in the direction of the ferry office and fell into step beside her.

Another shiver coursed through her. This one due more to dread at the coming encounter than to air temperature.

"Cold?"

The man didn't miss a thing.

"Yes. Not to mention nervous." She shook her head. "I'm striking out left and right with my nephew. And I'm running out of ideas."

He shrugged off his jacket and draped it over her shoulders. "You could send him home."

As warmth—and the scent that was all J.C.—seeped into her pores and invaded her senses, she lost her train of thought and her step faltered. "I can't…" The words rasped, and she stopped. Cleared her throat. Tried again. "I can't take your jacket."

The protest came out halfhearted, and she knew it. Based on the quick grin he flashed her, J.C. did, too. Putting his hand on the small of her back, he urged her forward.

"Too late. So why don't you send him home if he's becoming unmanageable?"

Heather bit back another protest about the jacket. She doubted it would do any good. Besides, wearing it made her feel safe. Protected. As did J.C.'s firm, steady hand at her back. An illusion, she knew. But she needed all the bolstering she could get.

"I was going to. I even called Susan to tell her that. In the end, though, I couldn't." She explained why.

"I see your problem." Creases appeared on J.C.'s brow. "If the group he's hanging around with is starting to dabble in drugs, he's on dangerous ground." He stopped and gestured toward the side of the ticket office. "He's at the rear. I'll stay close but out of sight while you talk to him."

Psyching herself up for the coming exchange, she nodded and stepped forward.

Her soft-soled shoes were noiseless on the pavement, giving Heather a chance to observe Brian without being noticed as she drew close. He was sitting on the concrete, his back against the wall of the building, arms wrapped around his drawn-up legs, chin resting on his knees. He'd put on a hooded jacket and pulled his backpack and suitcase close beside him.

Gone was the defiant glare. Gone was the palpable anger. Gone was the bravado. His shoulders were slumped, and he looked scared. And much more like the little boy she'd once known, who had loved to tag along with his aunt during family visits.

Her hope soared. Perhaps she'd be able to reach him after all.

Crossing her fingers, she stepped into his line of sight.

"Hi, Brian."

His head jerked toward her, and an instant later he sprang to his feet, his body rigid as he glared at her. "How did you find me?"

Her hope plummeted. In the space of a few heartbeats, the rebellious teen had returned.

"You can't run away, Brian." She avoided his question. "You're only thirteen."

"Right. I'm still a kid. I don't get any say in what happens in my life." Bitterness and frustration twisted his features. "Well, you know what? I'm tired of people telling me what to do. Watching over my shoulder. First mom, now you. Why can't everyone just leave me alone?"

His voice broke on the last word, and Heather felt the pressure of tears in her throat as he shifted away from her and dipped his head, his bangs falling into his eyes. She knew what it felt like to have your world turned upside down. To feel adrift. She'd reacted differently than Brian when her parents separated, coped in a different way. But the driving emotion behind her behavior had been the same.

"I'm sorry you feel that way, Brian. I know how hard it is to…"

"You don't know anything about what my life is like! Neither does Mom. Or that dumb counselor at school she made me talk to!"

His words came out muffled and choked. Heather

stepped closer, her heart aching. "Please, Brian, don't shut us out. We all want what's best for you. Getting involved with the wrong crowd can have repercussions that last a lifetime." She laid a hand on his arm. "Why don't you let…"

Swinging toward her, Brian shook off her touch. "Just leave me alone!"

Then he shoved her away.

Hard.

Caught off guard, Heather stumbled back a step. Her heel snagged on an uneven piece of concrete, and she struggled to maintain her balance as J.C.'s jacket slipped off her shoulders. Failing, she braced for the impact.

Instead of a hard landing on the unforgiving concrete, however, she found herself caught in a pair of strong arms and supported against a solid chest, the rapid thud of a heart pounding beneath her ear.

"Are you okay?"

As the husky words registered, she managed a shaky nod. "Yes."

J.C. settled her on her feet and gave her a quick inspection, then turned his attention to the teen standing a few feet away. Putting himself between Heather and her nephew, he planted his fists on his hips as he assessed the boy.

Though he was two years younger than Nathan had been when J.C. inherited responsibility for his younger brother, Brian exuded the same explosive anger. The same sense that the world hadn't treated him fairly. The same sullen attitude.

But this kid's veneer of defiance hadn't yet hardened into an impenetrable mask, as Nathan's had. J.C. could tell that by the slight quiver at the corners of his mouth. By the way he shoved his hands into his pockets and adopted a closed-in, protective posture. By the fear in his eyes.

Brian knew he was on dangerous ground. And he cared.

Nathan never had.

That was in this kid's favor. But no way did J.C. intend to let him off easy for shoving Heather. Brian might be only thirteen, but he was as tall as his aunt. Capable of hurting her.

That thought made J.C.'s blood run cold.

Moving in on the teen, he pinned him with a steely stare and planted his fists on his hips. Brian edged away until his back was up against the wall.

Invading his personal space, J.C. got close enough to smell his fear. "Let's get one thing straight, Brian. You never use physical force against another person no matter how angry you are—unless they're attacking you. Got it?"

When he didn't respond, J.C. braced his hands on the wall on either side of Brian's head and leaned even closer to his face. "Got it?"

Brian blinked. Swallowed. "Yeah."

J.C. held his position for a full ten seconds, then eased back slightly and folded his arms across his chest. "Now let me tell you why running away is a bad idea. Most of the time, I work in Chicago. In the back alleys, where runaways often end up. They sleep near Dumpsters, like you were going to do tonight. Or in cardboard sheds under bridges, down by the river. To survive, they end up doing things that aren't pretty. They get on the bad side of the law. They get hooked on drugs. A lot of them end up in prison…or dead. Sometimes the ones in prison *wish* they were dead."

He let that sink in for a minute, making sure Brian was listening. "A lot of those runaways don't have people who care about them. That's a tragedy, and I feel sorry for them. I *don't* feel sorry for you. So your parents split. There are worse things in life. Your mom and dad are still around, and they love you. Your aunt disrupted her own life to take you in after things got rough at home—because she cares. You're old enough to appreciate that kind of love and support. I suggest you start."

After several seconds, J.C. moved out of the kid's personal space and checked on Heather. She stood a few feet away, her arms wrapped around her body, the mist obscuring the nuances of her features. But he could tell she was shaking.

Retrieving his jacket from the ground, he moved beside her and draped it around her shoulders again, keeping his back to Brian.

"Are you okay taking him home?" He kept his volume low as he studied her. He didn't like the idea of her alone in the house with the angry kid behind him. Yet there wasn't a good alternative, short of putting Brian in the station's juvenile cell for the night. But that would involve legalities, which he suspected Heather wouldn't want to pursue.

"Yes."

He gave her an intent look. "I want you to promise you'll call me if you have any concern about your safety."

Shock parted her lips. "Brian wouldn't hurt me, J.C."

"He almost did tonight."

"It was an accident."

"Anger can be very dangerous."

"I'll be fine."

"I still want you to promise you'll call if anything raises an alarm."

She caught her lower lip between her teeth and gave a slow nod. "Okay."

"I'll walk you to your car." Stepping aside, he spoke to Brian as he picked up the teen's suitcase. "Let's go."

Brian reached for his backpack, slung it over one shoulder, and gave a wide berth to the two adults as he trudged toward the front of the building, his shoulders slumping.

Heather followed, and J.C. kept pace beside her during the silent walk through the fog to the end of the wharf.

When they reached her car, she opened the trunk.

Brian dumped his backpack inside and moved toward the front passenger door as J.C. added the suitcase and closed the lid.

After shrugging out of his jacket, Heather held it out. "Thank you for everything tonight."

Her voice was soft. So were her eyes, he noted, as he took the jacket. Her cold fingers brushed his, and the temptation to pull her close and wrap her in his arms, to keep her safe and warm, was strong. Very strong.

Instead, he took her hand and gave it a quick encouraging squeeze. "I wish I could do more." He checked on Brian, who was slouched in the front seat, and tried to focus on the problem at hand instead of the appealing woman a whisper away. "He's got some major attitude issues."

"I know. But he used to be a good kid. Susan says he still was up until the split a few months ago. Maybe time will fix the problem."

"If he doesn't get into serious trouble first."

"I'm hoping that for tonight he'll be too tired to do anything but sleep. I know I will be." She checked her watch and shook her head. "This is way past my bedtime."

"Will you be okay driving home in the fog?"

"I'm used to this weather. And I don't have far to go. Good night, J.C."

"Good night."

She slid into the driver's seat, and he shut the door behind her, backing up as she turned the key and put the car in gear. With a weary smile and wave, she drove into the night.

J.C. watched until the fog swallowed the tail-lights. Then he headed for his bike. Even though it was the first day of summer, the night was chilly, and the mist was seeping into his shirt.

As he approached his bike, he slid his arms into the sleeves of his jacket. It was still warm, and a faint sweet scent clung to it. Heather's scent. Lifting the collar, he tipped his head and inhaled. How odd that a fragrance could somehow ease the soul-deep loneliness that he'd come to accept as his destiny.

He could get used to having that scent—and the woman it belonged to—in his life, he realized.

But while Heather might be more approachable now than she'd been at their first meeting in the tearoom, and while he no longer thought of her as out of his league, one big stumbling block still stood in the path to any kind of relationship.

He was going to be around for only nine more weeks. And Heather's life was here, on Nantucket.

If there was any kind of future for the two of them, it was as obscure as the buildings along Main Street on this fog-shrouded night, J.C. mused as he took the cobblestones slow and easy. Only one person had a clear vision of his future, and He hadn't yet shared it with J.C.

But as he pedaled through the dark Nantucket streets in the still, empty hours after midnight when he always felt most alone, J.C. couldn't help wishing his tomorrows would include a lovely tearoom owner.

Chapter Eight

At eight-thirty the next morning, as J.C. turned onto Lighthouse Lane after finishing his night shift, Heather was just coming through her garden gate, a bouquet in hand.

Her jeans were damp at the knees, and there was a streak of dirt on her cheek. In the background, he caught a glimpse of a shovel leaning against a tree, a pair of garden gloves on the ground beside it.

Gliding to a stop beside her, he noted the shadows under her eyes and the tautness in her features. Souvenirs of last night—or indications of more trouble?

"Good morning." He balanced himself with one foot on the ground. "I thought you'd sleep in."

"I wish." She shook her head ruefully. "But I did manage to get about six hours."

"Any more problems?"

"No. I haven't seen Brian yet this morning. I

thought I'd do a little gardening while I planned my strategy. I got rid of the weeds, but unfortunately a strategy eluded me."

"Did he say anything last night, on the way home?"

"One sentence. 'I can't believe you called the cops.'" She shook her head. "I tried to explain that you were a neighbor, but he just turned away. I did ask about the missing money, and he handed it over. But he went straight to his room as soon we got back." She fingered the delicate petal of a yellow daylily and sighed.

J.C. wished he could offer her some guidance. But so far, his advice had done more harm than good.

"I'm sorry you have to deal with this, Heather. Reaching a kid with that much anger inside isn't easy."

"The thing is, I know how he feels." She touched the tip of a delicate, lacy fern. "When my parents split, it turned my life upside down, too. Everything in my safe, predictable little world changed. My life was spinning out of control, and I felt powerless. Brian's taking his frustration and anger and fear out on everyone and everything. I took mine out on the cause of the problem—my dad."

"Do you think he should do the same thing?"

Heather's features hardened. "Maybe. This *is* Peter's fault. He cheated on my sister. Multiple times. There was no trust left in that relationship by the time they separated."

"Does Brian know that?"

"Susan said she talked to him about it. But he doesn't care about the reasons for the split. He just wants things back the way they were. Like I did."

"Maybe it would help if you shared some of your own background with him."

She pursed her lips, and her expression grew thoughtful. "The empathetic approach. Do you think that might work?"

He gave a slight shrug and shook his head. "I haven't a clue. Empathy wasn't a tool I used with my siblings. Back in those days, I was living with perennial sleep deprivation while trying to cope with school, work and keeping tabs on Marci and Nathan. I didn't have much time or patience for psychological techniques—or tolerance for disruptive behavior, whatever the cause."

"Well, I think it's worth a try. Things can't get any worse than they are now."

That wasn't true, but J.C. saw no reason to add to her stress by voicing that thought.

"Listen…thanks again for all you did last night."

"No problem." He gestured toward the flowers. "Nice bouquet."

She smiled down at the colorful blossoms. "Nothing beats fresh flowers to brighten a day. I'm taking these over to Kate. She's laid up with a bad summer cold. See you later." Lifting her hand, she set off down the walk, toward her neighbor's house.

As he watched her, the rising sun peeked through the trees ahead, gilding her hair and bathing her slender form in a golden light. She was a beautiful woman, J.C. thought. Inside and out. Once again, despite her own problems, she was putting someone else first. Doing her best to offer some cheer to a person in need of a little pick-me-up.

A rush of tenderness washed over him, smoothing the blemishes from his soul much as the rising tide sweeps over the sand, removing debris and leaving a clean, fresh expanse in its wake.

And as he pushed off and pedaled toward his own tiny cottage to get some much-needed shut-eye after his busy night, he found himself hoping a certain tearoom owner would play a starring role in his dreams.

An hour later, holding a tray containing five fresh-baked blueberry muffins and two glasses of milk, Heather ascended the stairs to the second floor. If she was the praying type, she'd send a plea heavenward about now.

But in light of what had happened after her last informal request to the Almighty, she refrained.

Pausing outside Brian's door, she balanced the tray in one hand and knocked.

No response.

She knew he was in there, because she'd heard him moving around a few minutes earlier. She rapped again. "I'm coming in, Brian."

Twisting the knob, she gave the door a gentle push, waiting on the threshold as it swung open.

The teen was stretched out on top of the comforter, still dressed in the cargo pants and sweatshirt from the night before. He'd kicked off his shoes, and they lay beside the packed suitcase at the foot of the bed. He didn't look her way.

Please, God, help me find the words that will reach him!

The supplication echoed in her mind before she could snatch it back. Not that it mattered. God had probably tuned her out by now, anyway.

Stepping into the room, she set the tray on top of the dresser across from the foot of the bed. After putting a muffin she didn't want on a plate, she picked up a glass of milk and sat in the upholstered chair beside the door. From there she had a good view of Brian's stony profile.

"Help yourself to a muffin. They just came out of the oven."

He didn't respond as she put her milk on the small skirted table beside her.

A full minute ticked by in silence.

Finally, willing her voice to remain steady, she followed her instincts and went with the direct approach. "You know, I thought you were growing up. But refusing to talk to someone is pretty immature."

He didn't move a muscle as she broke off a piece of muffin. Put it in her mouth. Chewed.

It tasted like sawdust.

Just when she thought he was going to ignore her, he turned his head and gave her an accusatory look. "You don't talk to Grandpa."

Blindsided by his comeback, she fumbled for her milk and took a swig, trying to dislodge the muffin that had stuck halfway down her throat.

"That's different." It was a lame response, and she knew it.

The slight curl of Brian's lips before he refocused on the ceiling told her he did, too. "Right."

Trying to regain her footing, Heather squeezed a piece of the muffin into a hard, doughy ball. It felt like the lump in her stomach.

How had he managed to turn her words around on her? Refusing to talk to someone *was* immature—unless there were good reasons. And she had plenty of those when it came to her father. Brian's refusal to talk to her, on the other hand, was based on guilt by association. He was mad at his mom for sending him to Nantucket, and Heather was her ally. The situations were completely different.

Weren't they?

Of course they were, she assured herself.

But his comment did give her the opening she needed to try the empathy tactic she and J.C. had discussed.

"Actually, I wanted to talk to you about your grandfather and me." Somehow, despite her nervousness, she managed to maintain an even, conversational tone.

He didn't say anything, but he did give her a wary look.

"When I was fourteen, my mom and dad split, just like yours did. Not only that, but Mom and I moved here, which turned my whole world upside down. I left behind the house I'd always lived in, all my friends and all the places I liked to hang out. I felt like my whole life was out of control, and I was very angry."

She set the glass back on the table. "My dad did what your dad has done many times. He broke his vow to remain true to his wife. That changed my life forever. Thanks to him, I ended up here, away from everything I knew."

"But you like it here."

That was true, Heather acknowledged. She couldn't imagine living anywhere else. Now. But that was beside the point. "I didn't in the beginning. The thing is, Brian, it's normal to be mad when people disrupt your life. I know exactly how you feel, because I've been there."

"Then how come Mom doesn't get it? Grandpa's her dad, too. I don't think she ever felt this way."

"She was already away at college, creating her own life apart from the family, when everything fell apart. So the breakup didn't affect her as much."

He shifted onto his side, propped his elbow on the pillow and rested his head in his hand, a frown creasing his brow. "I guess I should be mad at Dad, like you are at Grandpa. But I don't want to be mad at him. He's always been a good father, you know?"

Yes, she did. Walter Anderson had been a good father, too. Unlike a lot of dads, whose business commitments seemed to take precedence over family, he'd always been there for the events in the lives of his daughters. School plays, soccer games, piano recitals. Even report card conferences. He'd never failed to show up.

All at once, a long-buried memory from her eighth-grade father/daughter dance surfaced. The two of them had practiced dance steps in the kitchen for weeks, her father patiently helping her master a few basic moves despite her thirteen-year-old gawkiness. She'd been confident they would impress everyone.

Instead, during the opening dance, she'd tripped in her brand-new first pair of heels and plopped on her bottom before her dad could save her.

She'd been mortified. Had begged her father to take her home. But he'd guided her into a quiet corner, and while she dabbed at her eyes with his handkerchief, he'd given her some advice.

"What happened out there isn't the end of the world, Heather. Most mistakes aren't. You have to learn from them, let them go and try again. Most of the time you'll get another chance to make them right."

And after coaxing her back onto the dance floor, he'd ended up salvaging the evening.

That was the kind of dad he'd been. And Heather had loved him for that. Respected him. Looked up to him.

Perhaps that was why his betrayal had hurt so much.

And why she'd never been able to forgive him.

"So should I be mad at Dad?"

Brian's question pulled her back to the present. Reminding her that this conversation was about him, not her.

Stuffing the memory back into a corner of her heart, she considered her answer. It would be easy to say yes. And a specific focus for his anger might be helpful. Peter deserved his enmity after what he'd done to destroy his family.

But for some reason, she couldn't bring herself to offer that advice.

"You don't have to be mad at anybody, Brian. But you need to try to understand why your mom did what she did. When people get married, they promise to stay true. They trust each other to honor that vow. After someone breaks it, the trust goes away. And it's very hard to rebuild that. Maybe it can be done if it happens once. But it happened more than that with your dad."

"Yeah. Mom told me." He traced the pattern on the comforter with his finger. "Why did he have to do that, anyway? Everything was so good before."

"Some people find temptation hard to resist. I guess that's what happened with your dad. But getting into trouble isn't going to make things better for you, Brian." She leaned forward. "Your mom told me that some of the guys you were hanging around with at home just got busted for marijuana possession."

His head jerked up, and his eyes widened. "I never did anything like that."

"That's good to know. But if you'd been with them when they got caught, you'd be in big trouble. Trouble that could affect the rest of your life. None of us want that to happen. And we'll do whatever we can to help you get through this tough time. Because we love you, Brian."

He blinked and once again dipped his chin to study the comforter. "That's what that cop said last night. Among other things."

Heather hadn't heard every word J.C. had spoken to Brian when he'd had the teen pinned against the wall, but she wasn't surprised he'd given him some straight talk. He wasn't the type to beat around the bush.

"I'd listen to him if I were you. He's seen plenty on the street. Before he came here, he was an undercover detective in a pretty tough neighborhood in Chicago. And he's been responsible for his younger brother and sister since he was eighteen. I know he had some problems with his brother when he was your age. So he knows what he's talking about."

Brian digested that. "He told me I needed to get a handle on my anger."

"That's good advice."

"I don't know how to do that." He blinked and swiped at his eyes. "Sometimes I wake up in the middle of the night and my stomach's in knots. All I want to do is get up and break things."

Heather reached over and touched his arm. "I'll tell you what. While you're here, if you start to feel that way, come and find me. No matter what time it is. And we'll try a hug instead, okay?"

He lifted one shoulder. "Yeah. I guess."

"You want to start now?"

"I'm not mad."

Heather smiled. "You can hug when you're happy, too."

Rising, she set her plate on the chair and moved to the bed. Sitting beside him, she held out her arms.

He hesitated. But only for a second. Then he sat up and leaned over to give her an awkward bear hug with his gangly adolescent arms. "I'm sorry about breaking your cups, Aunt Heather. And for shoving you last night."

The words were muffled against her shoulder, but Heather heard them loud and clear. And the coil of tension that had been building inside her since his arrival began to unwind.

"We'll make a fresh start, okay?"

"Okay."

He released her, and she stood to gesture toward the tray on the dresser. "I'd hate for those blueberry muffins to go to waste."

"I thought you said no food in the room?"

She smiled. "There are always exceptions." She

picked up her plate and sat back in the chair by the door. "I brought five. And I've had a head start." She took a bite out of her muffin.

Brian grinned and swung his legs to the floor. "I eat fast."

As he moved to the tray and plopped two muffins on a plate, Heather chewed the bite she'd taken.

And this time she had no difficulty swallowing it.

If all continued to go well, maybe there would be smoother sailing ahead.

J.C. yawned and stretched. He had an hour before he had to report for the night shift. A good opportunity to jot his weekly note to Nathan. Although Marci might be right, and Nathan might be pitching them, unopened, if nothing else their steady arrival would remind him that someone cared. And was thinking about him. That, and prayer, was about all he could do for his brother at this point.

A gust of wind rattled the shutters on his cottage, and rain hammered on the roof. It should be a quiet night crimewise, he reflected as he retrieved some notepaper. Even troublemakers wouldn't be inclined to venture out into this storm.

Just as he sat down at the café table and picked up his pen, a flash of lightning strobed the sky. The lights flickered, followed by a splintering noise. Moments later, the explosive sound of shattering glass ripped through the night.

And it was close.

Very close.

Springing to his feet, J.C. opened his door and peered outside. Edith's house looked okay, from what he could see through the darkness and slashing rain. He leaned farther out and checked on The Devon Rose.

As he did so, another flash of lightning illuminated the sky.

The breath jammed in his throat.

A large piece of the towering maple tree in Heather's garden had been sheared off and had fallen against the house. Her bedroom window had been obliterated. And obviously broken.

J.C. had no idea how the furniture in the room was arranged, but if her bed was anywhere near that window, the broken glass could have…

He cut off that line of thought. Speculation was useless. Instead, he shoved the door shut behind him and sprinted out of Edith's yard, heading toward the entrance to The Devon Rose.

He covered the distance in record time, yet as he pounded on her door, every second felt like an eternity.

When at last it was thrown open by Brian, the teen's pallor and panicked greeting sent his pulse skyrocketing.

"Aunt Heather's bleeding."

Without a word, he ran past Brian and took the steps two at a time, zeroing in on the only lighted room on the left side of the hall.

When he reached the doorway, the first thing he noted was that the bed wasn't next to the window. That was the good news.

The bad news was that Heather was standing on one foot at the end of it, clutching the bedpost, while blood dripped past her bare toes and formed a growing red puddle on the hardwood floor.

A sudden gust of wind blew in the window, bringing with it a spray of rain—and galvanizing him into action.

"Brian, go get me a clean hand towel." He issued the command over his shoulder as he strode into the room, shards of glass crunching beneath his shoes.

Heather blinked at him, her shell-shocked expression similar to ones he'd often seen on the faces of trauma victims. "J.C.... What are you doing here?"

"I heard the crash, and when I saw the tree against the house, I ran over." He dropped to the balls of his feet beside her. "Bend your knee."

She did as he instructed, and he cradled the top of her foot in his hand as he examined the sole.

"I was sleeping when the tree came through the window. I g-guess I wasn't thinking straight when I got up. I should have realized there would be glass all over the floor. Pretty d-dumb, huh?" She tried to joke, but a telltale quiver ran through her voice.

"Is this okay?" Brian appeared at his shoulder and thrust a towel at him.

J.C. took it. "Yeah."

There was too much blood to assess the cut on her heel, so he wrapped her foot in the towel, tucked the end under and stood. "I need to wash this off and get a look at it in better light. Where's the bathroom?"

"At the end of the hall," Brian offered.

Heather started to put her foot on the floor, but J.C. restrained her with a touch. "Not a good idea until we see how deep that is. I'll carry you down there."

A flicker of panic sparked in her eyes, and she eased back slightly, as she'd done in their early encounters. "I can walk."

He gentled his tone and tried for a smile. "Be practical, Heather. I'd hate to have you bleeding all the way down the hall, and that's what might happen if the cut's deep." He saw her resolve wavering. "Come on. It's not every day I get to rescue a damsel in distress." He winked, trying to put her at ease as he moved closer. "Put your arm around my neck."

She hesitated, then complied.

Bending, he tucked one arm under her knees and the other under her back as he swept her up against his chest.

Her eyes widened. "You're wet."

She was right. His black T-shirt was clinging to him like a second skin. "Sorry. It's pouring outside, and I didn't stop for a jacket."

With her arms looped around his neck, and her face mere inches away, J.C. saw several things he'd never noticed before. She had a very faint but endearing sprinkling of freckles across her nose. There were little flecks of green in her hazel irises. And her lips looked full, soft—and eminently kissable.

Clearing his throat, he yanked his gaze away and strode down the hall. Needing a distraction, he turned his attention to Brian. There were headphones around the teen's neck, the cord dangling down the front of the T-shirt he wore over his gym shorts. And he was still way too pale.

"Would you get the bathroom light for me, Brian? And find me a clean washcloth?"

The teen hurried ahead and flipped the light switch, moving out of the way as J.C. went through the door sideways and set Heather carefully on a small vanity chair. She was trembling now. From reaction? Shock? Cold?

It could be the latter, he speculated, taking in her attire for the first time. She wore some sort of knee-length peach-colored thing, with a modest neckline and skinny straps that bared her shoulders—and shimmered every time she breathed.

Yeah, that could make her cold.

But it was having the opposite effect on him.

Focus, J.C., focus, he reminded himself sternly.

Brian reappeared with the washcloth, and J.C. moved to the sink to rinse his hands. Toweling them dry, he cleaned the blood off Heather's foot and assessed the cut on her heel.

"How bad is it?" She still sounded shaky.

"Long but not too deep. We can go to the E.R. if you want to, but I don't think it will need stitches if I bandage it well. Do you have any first-aid supplies?"

"Yes. Downstairs, in the cabinet next to the kitchen sink. I'd rather try that. I'm not in the mood to spend hours in the E.R."

"I'll get them," Brian offered.

"Thanks." J.C. gave him a quick smile.

As the teen exited, J.C. raised an eyebrow at Heather and lowered his voice. "Do I detect a change in attitude? Or is it a temporary improvement due to the emergency?"

"We had a long talk this morning." She glanced toward her foot, which remained cradled in his hand, and swallowed. "I shared how I felt when my parents broke up, and that seems to have opened the lines of communication."

The sound of someone bounding up the stairs cut off their conversation, and seconds later Brian appeared, carrying a large plastic box with a red cross on the top.

"See if there's some kind of antiseptic ointment in there," J.C. instructed. He could do it himself, but he was enjoying the delicate feel of Heather's foot in his hand. "We also need gauze and tape. And butterfly bandages, if you find any. They'll be labeled."

After rummaging around, the teen withdrew all the items J.C. had asked for, including several packets of the specialty bandages.

"Good," J.C. praised. "Now wash your hands. I'll need your help."

As the teen complied, J.C. applied antiseptic to the cut and opened three of the bandages. When Brian was ready, J.C. eased the edges of the laceration together. "I need you to hold your aunt's foot like this while I put the bandages on."

Brian did as instructed while J.C. positioned the bandages. Afterward, he stepped aside to watch as J.C. covered the cut with a sterile pad and secured it in place with roller gauze.

"Is there any aspirin or pain reliever in there?" J.C. tipped his head toward the first-aid supplies.

"Yes." Heather leaned over to rummage through the box, withdrawing a bottle.

"I'd advise taking some. This may begin to throb." Without waiting for a reply, he pulled a paper cup out of the dispenser beside the sink, filled it with water and handed it to her. "Do you have any sheets of plastic? I'll block that window off for you as best I can."

Heather downed the aspirin. "Aren't you on nights this week?"

"Yes." He checked his watch. He was supposed to be on duty in half an hour. "I think I can get a thirty-minute reprieve. It shouldn't take longer than that to get the window covered if Brian helps. You willing?" He turned toward the teen.

"Yeah. Sure."

"There's some plastic in the basement," Heather

said. "Near the furnace. I'm sorry to put you to all this trouble, J.C."

"No problem. Is there another bedroom you can sleep in?"

"My mom's room. It's next to the bathroom, on the other side of the hall."

"Let's get you settled before we work on the window." Leaning down, he once more swung her up into his arms. "No walking on this foot until tomorrow, okay? I'll check it for you when I get off duty."

He couldn't help noticing that the bodice of her gown was shimmering like crazy, thanks to her shallow, rapid respiration. And a man could get lost in those tender, appealing eyes…

"J.C.?"

She must have asked him a question, he realized as warmth surged up his neck. "Sorry. I missed that."

"I said you'd better put me down fast, or you'll get a hernia."

He attempted a smile as he eased her through the door. "No chance of that. You're a lightweight."

Who could nevertheless play havoc with his metabolism, he conceded.

After settling her in her mother's room, he and Brian went to work on the window. They managed to cut off most of the branches sticking into the room, and J.C. was satisfied that the plastic they taped up to seal off the window would hold for a few hours.

While Brian swept the floor, J.C. did his best to clean up the blood. He had a pretty high tolerance for gore, but for some reason, his stomach was revolting tonight.

"I don't think that's gonna come off."

At Brian's comment, J.C. gave the spot one last scrub. Despite his best efforts, a slight dark stain remained. Perhaps it always would.

"You may be right. Blood is hard to clean up."

"I bet you see a lot of it in your job."

An image of the warehouse on the fateful day of the drug bust flitted through his mind. There had been plenty of blood that day. Jack and Scott had been lying in spreading pools of it while he had taken cover behind some crates as bullets whizzed around him. He'd been close enough to watch the life seep out of them. Close enough to reach out and touch them. But helpless to provide any assistance.

His stomach clenched, and he cleared his throat. "Some."

"Aunt Heather says you're a detective."

"That's right."

"That must be pretty cool."

He hated to disillusion the boy, but "cool" was hardly the way he'd describe his job. "Not always." Rising, he wiped his hands on the rag. "I'm going to check on your aunt and then head to work. You can lock up after me."

Detouring to the bathroom, J.C. added the bloody

rag to the towel and washcloth in the tub before stepping into the darkened room where Heather lay.

"I'm still awake, J.C."

That might be true, but the slight slur to her words suggested sleep was about to claim her.

"I'm heading out. We'll deal with the tree and the window in the morning."

"Okay. Thank you again."

She extended her hand, and he moved forward to give it a slight squeeze.

But that wasn't good enough.

On impulse, he leaned down and brushed his lips over her forehead. "Sleep well."

Before she could respond, he left the room.

Brian was waiting for him by the front door, and a flash of lightning zigzagged outside the window as he approached.

"Is she gonna be okay?"

"Yes. It's a bad cut, but it should heal without any problem. She might need a little more help than usual around here for a few days, though. Are you okay with that?"

"Yeah."

"I'll be back tomorrow. Thanks for pitching in tonight."

The boy's complexion reddened. "I didn't do anything."

"Yes, you did. I couldn't have handled this without another set of hands, and you were there when I needed you." J.C. opened the door and stepped through. "See you tomorrow."

As the lock clicked into place behind him, he once more sprinted through the driving rain toward his cottage, hoping the raging storm would wreak no more havoc this night.

But in truth he was more concerned about the storm now raging within. Thanks to the moments he'd held Heather in his arms.

She'd felt good there, nestled against his chest. And right. As if it was where she belonged.

And that kind of sentiment was dangerous with a capital *D,* he reminded himself as another bolt of lightning strafed the sky. He didn't need—or want—any more complications in his life.

Meaning that kiss had been a big mistake.

So why had he done it?

Not liking the answer that popped to mind, J.C. did his best to quash it.

Nevertheless, its aftereffects reverberated in his heart much like the distant rumble of thunder, leaving him feeling as unsettled as the stormy Nantucket night.

Chapter Nine

Someone was watching her.

Through a haze of sleep, Heather sensed the scrutiny and struggled to push aside the dulling effects of slumber. But it wasn't easy. It had taken her hours to drift off last night after all the excitement. Particularly those moments in J.C.'s arms…and that brush of his lips across her forehead. Throw in a foot that throbbed every time she moved, and she doubted she'd gotten more than four hours of restless sleep.

Forcing her eyes open at last, she blinked against the bright sunshine peeking in through the lace curtains. Edith stood in the doorway, Brian hovering behind her.

"You're awake." The older woman came into the room and planted herself beside the bed. Brian was right behind her.

"I am now." She stifled a yawn. "What are you doing here?"

"She came to the back door when I went down to get a muffin, so I let her in," Brian offered.

"J.C. called early this morning." Edith picked up the narrative. "Chester and I were at that benefit for the Atheneum last night and didn't even know about all your excitement until he called and woke us up. At *six-thirty.* Sounds like he came to the rescue. A regular knight in shining armor." She gave Heather a satisfied smile.

"He was awesome," Brian verified.

Edith's smile turned smug.

"He was very neighborly." Heather emphasized the last word and changed the subject. "So what are you doing here?"

"Chester lined up a tree removal crew to get rid of that branch for you. The chain saw should kick in in five minutes, and I didn't want you to be startled in case you were still sleeping. Also, I already called the glass company. They'll be here later this morning. And since Kate still has a cold and canceled her charters for the day, I don't have to watch the girls. That means I can help out with tea this afternoon. You need to favor that foot. J.C. said it was a bad cut."

"I thought you had a tai chi class on Friday afternoons?"

Edith waved the comment aside. "I'm glad to have an excuse to skip it. I don't know why I let Mary Lou Hawkins talk me into signing up for it. She says it's supposed to reduce stress, but it's way too slow-paced if you ask me."

A smile twitched at Heather's lips. "I think that's the point."

"Hmph. Give me jazzy step aerobics any day."

The chain saw roared to life outside, and Edith consulted her watch. "Eight o'clock on the dot. Right on time. I better get out there and help Chester supervise. You take it easy this morning, and I'll be back this afternoon."

The older woman bustled out the door, energy crackling in her wake.

Brian turned to Heather. "Wow. Is she always like that?"

"You mean like a human tornado?"

"Yeah."

"Pretty much. But she has a heart of gold, and I couldn't get along without her. How about some breakfast?"

He gave her a skeptical look. "The cop said you weren't supposed to move around a lot."

Heather bristled. She was glad Brian respected J.C.'s opinion, but she wasn't about to be coddled. "I'm not going to overdo it. But I don't plan to stay in bed all day, either."

"I just had a muffin." Brian stuck his hands in his pockets. "Maybe we could have breakfast in an hour or two. You could rest until then."

Was her nephew sincerely concerned? Heather wondered. Or buying time, hoping J.C. would show up in the interim and take charge of the situation again, as he had last night?

But she wasn't in the mood to get up yet, anyway. Why fight the general consensus? "Okay. That sounds good. I'll make waffles later."

He grinned. "The ones I used to like, with the nuts?"

"I think that could be arranged."

The chain saw started up again, and Heather cringed. She didn't even want to know what kind of destruction the storm had inflicted on her house—or her garden. And for the next hour or two, she intended to do her best to put it out of her mind.

"Shut the door when you leave, okay?"

Brian complied, and Heather settled back against her pillow. She didn't expect to sleep, but much to her surprise, her eyelids drifted closed despite the noise.

When she opened them again, an hour and a half had passed. And all was quiet. Meaning it was time to assess the damage.

Swinging her legs to the floor, she stood, gingerly putting her weight on the ball of her injured foot. Good. It didn't hurt too much. She could maneuver like this for a couple of days without much problem.

As she limped toward her room, holding on to the wall for support, she tried to steel herself for the mess inside—and out.

But much to her surprise, her room was largely intact. Almost every trace of last night's incident had been erased. Except for the clear plastic over the window, the room looked just as it had for the past twenty years. Same pale blue walls. Same lace curtains. Same white wicker dresser, with a wicker-framed mirror centered above. The bed boasted the same polished brass headboard. The familiar blue-and-white floral chair occupied one corner, the skirt ruffled, the back tufted.

Heather hadn't paid much attention to her room decor in years. Yet all at once it seemed stale. And juvenile. No surprise there, she supposed. The room had been designed for a fourteen-year-old. She was now thirty-four, and her tastes had matured. Where once she'd worn frilly clothes, she now favored sleek lines and classic looks. This room didn't reflect that evolution. Why had she never noticed that?

But perhaps the more pertinent question was, why was she noticing it now?

Pushing that troubling puzzle aside, she limped over to the window. Her time could be put to better use evaluating the damage in her garden, she told herself.

Although the plastic distorted her view, she could tell the storm had taken a toll on her private haven. One side of a boxwood triangle bore deep indentations, and the begonias inside had been crushed. Leaves littered the walkway, and her birdbath was slightly askew.

What a mess.

And with her foot problem, it would be days before she could repair the damage.

Disheartened, she was about to turn away when a movement below caught her attention. Shifting position, she spotted J.C. He was wearing jeans and another chest-hugging black T-shirt, she noted. Similar to the one that had sent her pulse skittering and made her respiration go haywire last night.

Like it was doing again.

While she recognized that reaction as a pure physical response, what she saw next touched her at a deep emotional level.

He was carrying a flat of begonias and a trowel. And as she watched, he stepped over the battered boxwood border, knelt and began to methodically repopulate the decimated patch with new plants.

After working a full night shift, J.C. was restoring her sanctuary instead of sleeping.

Wow.

As he dug into the fertile earth and gently mounded dirt around each new plant, tears began to roll down her cheeks.

Rubbing them away with the backs of her hands, Heather tried to attribute her emotional response to a delayed reaction to last night's trauma.

Yet deep inside she knew better.

J.C.'s thoughtful, unselfish gesture had touched a place deep inside her. And dislodged a huge chunk of the wall she'd built around her heart.

A few weeks ago, when Julie had told her there were still some good guys out there, Heather had blown her off.

But she was beginning to think that maybe…just maybe…the man in her garden might be one of them.

"Would you like some coffee?"

As Heather asked the question, J.C. shifted his weight from one knee to the other and looked over his shoulder. His slow smile was as warming as the Nantucket summer sun.

"Good morning."

The deep, mellow timbre of his greeting did nothing to stabilize her unruly pulse.

"Good morning." She ventured a few steps closer and perused her garden. In the ten minutes it had taken her to throw on a pair of jeans and a T-shirt, he'd managed to plant more than half of the begonias. "I saw you from the window. How did you know what to buy?"

"I swung by here at dawn, while I was on patrol, to look over the damage. I picked these up on my way home." He gestured to the flat of begonias. "I also checked the boxwood. None of them are broken to the ground, so I assume they'll fill back out eventually. However, what I know about gardening would fit in a teacup." He gave her that appealing half-hitch grin.

"Boxwoods are pretty hardy." She folded her arms across her chest. "After all you've done for me over the past few days, I don't even know how to begin to thank you."

"I was glad to help. I've been in tough spots myself. How's the foot?"

"Not too bad."

"I'll check it out as soon as I'm done here."

"Is there anything you don't know how to deal with?"

When a flash of pain echoed in the depths of his dark eyes, Heather cringed. Of all the stupid comments! She knew how he felt about his failures with his siblings.

"I'm sorry, J.C. I meant that as a compliment."

"I know. It's okay." His smile didn't quite reach his eyes. "Did I hear you offer coffee? At The Devon Rose?"

His abrupt change of subject told Heather it wasn't okay. But she didn't know how to make amends.

Pasting on a smile of her own, she tucked her hands in the pockets of her jeans. "I make exceptions on rare occasions."

"Then the answer is yes."

"How do you take it?"

"Straight and strong."

Sort of like the man, Heather reflected. "Coming right up."

As she pivoted toward the back door, an idea occurred to her, and she paused. The gesture wouldn't atone for her insensitive remark, but it would help salve her conscience.

Half turning toward him, she tucked her hair

behind her ear. "I promised Brian I'd make whole-wheat pecan waffles for breakfast. Would you like to join us?"

The invitation seemed to surprise him, and when he hesitated, she backed off. "It's okay if you don't want to. You must be tired after working all night, and this—" she swept her hand over the garden "—has already eaten into your sleep time."

He sat back on his heels and regarded her. She was certain he was going to refuse, but now it was his turn to surprise her. "I'd like that. I haven't had homemade waffles in years."

"Okay. Good. How long do you need out here?"

"Half an hour?"

"That works. I'll have Brian bring your coffee out when it's ready."

As Heather limped back into the house, she was already regretting the impulsive invitation. Logic told her she should be backing away from J.C., not encouraging interaction.

All she had to do was add up the facts. He'd kissed her last night. The chemistry between them was potent. She was breaking her vow about keeping her distance from eligible men. He was leaving in a few weeks.

The sum of all that could be heartbreak.

Yet J.C. had tapped into a deep vein of loneliness she hadn't even known existed. And he'd infused her life with new warmth, adding a spark to days that had become as predictable and stale as her bedroom furnishings.

The temptation to explore the mutual attraction was strong. And her heart told her to go for it. To trust her instincts.

But those instincts had misled her once, with Mark.

How could she be sure they wouldn't do so again?

"These are great, Aunt Heather." Brian stabbed his last piece of waffle with his fork and ran it around his plate, sopping up as much of the remaining syrup as possible.

"I second that." J.C. smiled at Heather and leaned back in his chair, cradling his mug in his hands—and feeling more relaxed than he had in a very long time.

"I'm glad you both enjoyed them." She rose from the small table in the corner of the kitchen and moved to the stove, where she added more hot water to her mug.

"If you have some extra house paint, I'll borrow Chester's ladder and touch up the siding before I turn in," J.C. offered, sipping his coffee.

"You don't have to do that." Heather slid back into her seat. "I've taken advantage of you too much already."

"I don't feel taken advantage of." He gave her a steady look, catching an endearing blush of color on her cheeks as she dropped her chin to fiddle with her tea bag.

"I could help."

At Brian's comment, J.C. switched his attention to the teen. Heather's nephew hadn't said much during the meal, despite J.C.'s attempts to draw him out. At first he'd suspected the boy's belligerent attitude was making a comeback. But as the meal progressed, Brian had seemed more shy than surly.

"Have you done much painting?"

"A little. My mom and I painted our porch in the spring."

This would be an opportunity for Brian to interact with a police officer on a friendly basis, J.C. mused. To show the teen his negative attitude toward law enforcement was misplaced.

"I could use the help. That okay with you, Heather?"

After a brief hesitation, Heather seemed to come to the same conclusion. "Sure. It will get done a lot quicker with two sets of hands. Thank you."

J.C. drained his mug. "Let's take a look at that foot first. Brian, you want to get the first-aid kit?" Standing, he moved to the sink to wash his hands.

"It feels okay," Heather protested.

"We still need to change the dressing. The last thing you want is an infection." He spoke over his shoulder as he adjusted the faucet.

Silence greeted his comment. When he returned to the table and scooted his chair closer to hers, however, Heather swiveled toward him, conceding his point by lifting her foot.

Positioning it on his jeans-clad knee, J.C. unwrapped the bandage as Brian watched over his shoulder.

"How does it look?" Heather asked.

"It bled a little more during the night, but there's no inflammation. Brian, would you hand me a clean sterile pad and the roll of gauze?"

The teen complied, hovering close as J.C. rebandaged the wound.

"Where did you learn to do this kind of stuff?" There was a touch of awe in the boy's tone.

"On-the-job training, for the most part. You have to know a little about a lot of things when you're a cop."

He'd also learned a lot because of his brother, J.C. reflected. Nathan had been in his share of street fights, and J.C. had hauled him home, beat-up and bleeding, more times than he cared to remember. Going to the E.R. would have raised too many questions. So he'd armed himself with bargain-bin first-aid books and dealt with as much as he could on his own.

J.C. finished dressing the cut and smiled at Heather, resting his hand lightly on her instep. "You okay?"

"Yes. It doesn't hurt much."

"It will help if you keep most of the weight on the ball of your foot. And if you stay off your feet as much as possible for a couple of days."

"Edith is going to help serve the tea this afternoon."

"Good." Gently lowering her foot on the floor, J.C. stood. "You ready to paint, Brian?"

"Yes."

J.C. picked up his plate. "Let's clear things up in here first and—"

Heather stopped him with a hand on his arm. "I'll deal with this. You guys handle the painting."

J.C. considered pushing, but the slight tilt to her chin told him to let it go. A sense of control was important to her, and that had already been badly compromised. At least she could still be in charge in her kitchen.

"Okay. I'll go get Chester's ladder. Brian, you round up the paint and some brushes."

Exiting through the back door, J.C. gave his handiwork a once-over as he passed the garden on the way to the gate. The brick paths had been swept; the begonias replaced; the birdbath resettled on its base. Except for the battered boxwoods, order had been restored to Heather's haven.

He wished he could restore it to her life as well.

And, truth be told, to his.

Because thanks to an appealing woman with warm, caring eyes, he felt more uncertain about his future now than when he'd stepped off the ferry three weeks ago.

"Aunt Heather, can I get some sodas?"

After adding a swirl of whipped cream to a miniature key lime tart, Heather straightened up, weighing the pastry bag in her hand.

"Sure. How are you guys doing?" They'd been

working on the house for an hour, and she'd been about to go out and check on them.

"Good. We're almost done. J.C. knows a lot about painting, too."

So it was J.C. now, Heather noted. Not "the cop." That was a good sign.

As Brian retrieved two cans of soda from the fridge, he spoke over his shoulder. "Did you know his brother is in prison?"

A shock wave rippled through her. J.C. had said he'd had some trouble with his kid brother, but she'd never guessed it was that serious.

"No. I didn't."

"Yeah. He's doing ten years for armed robbery. J.C. says Nathan—that's his name—started hanging around with a gang when he was a kid. J.C. used to go out looking for him at night in the streets. Nathan was into some serious stuff that really messed up his life. I think J.C. feels real bad about it. But he tried, you know? His brother just wouldn't listen."

Heather was still processing that information when Brian switched topics.

"Can we go swimming on your day off on Monday, Aunt Heather? J.C. says there's a cool beach you like to go to."

She'd proposed that idea the day Brian arrived, and he'd turned up his nose. She supposed the heart-to-heart talk the two of them had had yesterday might be partly responsible for his new amenability. But she suspected a good chunk of the credit went to her temporary next-door neighbor, who seemed to have gained a loyal fan.

Meaning she owed him. Big-time.

"A beach trip sounds good to me. We could take a picnic lunch."

"Cool." Brian breezed toward the back door. Stopping on the threshold, he looked back. "J.C.'s off that day, too. Could I ask him to come with us?"

Heather's grip tightened on the pastry bag, and it spewed a snake of whipped cream across the stainless-steel prep table.

Grabbing a dishcloth, she wiped up the mess as she wrestled with Brian's request. Her first inclination was to say no. A picnic on the beach with J.C. sounded way too cozy.

On the other hand, this was the most enthusiasm her nephew had shown since his arrival. If he was turning a corner, she didn't want to jinx it. And being in J.C.'s company was obviously good for him.

Bottom line, saying no might be safe—but it would also be selfish.

"You can ask, Brian. But he might have other things to do."

She hoped.

"Yeah. I know. But maybe he can come for a while." Pushing through the door, he clattered down the porch steps.

Fifteen minutes later, as Heather sat on a stool

beside the prep table, lamenting over a tray of petits fours that had been decorated with less than her usual precision, J.C. knocked on the screen door.

"May I come in?"

Her pulse took a leap as his broad shoulders filled her doorway. Annoyed, she did her best to rein it in as she forced a smile. "Of course. All done?"

"Yes." He stepped inside but remained near the door, keeping a distance between them. "Brian is cleaning the brushes."

"Thanks again for everything."

He dismissed her gratitude with a shrug. "I was glad to help. Listen…are you okay with this picnic thing on Monday?"

She wiped her hands on her apron. "It would be good for Brian, if you can spare the time. You seem to be a positive influence on him."

He slid his palms into the back pockets of his jeans, pulling the black T-shirt taut across his broad chest. Heather's gaze dropped for an instant before she jerked it back up to his face.

"I have the time. But you didn't answer my question."

Taking a deep breath, she decided to be honest. "I'm a little concerned."

"About what?"

"You make me nervous."

"Why?"

She tucked her hair behind her ear. "I'm beginning to like you…too much."

A flicker of surprise flashed through his eyes. Then they darkened. "The feeling is mutual—as you probably figured out after that kiss last night. And as long as we're being frank, I'm no more thrilled by this development than you are. I know you aren't in the market for a relationship…especially with someone who won't be here very long. And I didn't come to Nantucket looking for romance. My life is complicated enough already."

Heather wasn't surprised J.C. had met her candor with a healthy dose of his own. That was yet another quality she admired in him. Rather than play games or dance around issues, he addressed them head-on.

"So where does that leave us?"

He folded his arms across his chest and propped his shoulder against the side of a cabinet. "We could avoid each other. But that means I'd have to avoid Brian, too—just when he seems to be coming around." He assessed her with those dark, intense eyes. "I can handle a day at the beach together if you can. It's not as if it's a date."

"That's true." Some of Heather's tension dissipated.

"I can also promise not to push you in directions you prefer not to go."

Her tension eased a few more notches. "In that case, I'm fine with it."

"Okay." He straightened up. "What time is good for you?"

"How about eleven?"

"That works. What can I bring?"

"Nothing. I'll just throw a few sandwiches together."

"All right. See you then."

Pushing through the door, he disappeared around the house as he headed toward the garden.

For a good two minutes, Heather remained on the stool, chin propped in hand. She was glad they'd acknowledged their mutual attraction. It was silly—and awkward—to try to ignore it. They weren't teens in the throes of their first crush, after all. Kids prey to their hormones. They were adults, with the maturity to manage the spark between them.

Besides, as long as they confined their interaction to activities that involved Brian, there'd be no chance for anything romantic to develop. They'd be safe.

But even as Heather assured herself of that, a disturbing little voice in the back of her mind whispered otherwise.

And no matter how hard she tried, she couldn't manage to silence it.

Chapter Ten

~

"Is this the beach express?"

At J.C.'s question, Heather leaned around the trunk of her car, where she was stowing the cooler. He was dressed much as he'd been on his first visit to Ladies Beach, she noted—in a gray Titan Tigers T-shirt and black swimming trunks that exposed his long, muscular legs.

Even though she'd reminded herself all weekend that this was a causal excursion, not a date, and even though she'd thought she had her emotions under control, her pulse kicked up a notch.

"This is it." She did her best to sound calm and cool. "Where'd you get that?" She gestured toward the foam bodyboard tucked under his arm, next to a rolled-up beach towel.

"I borrowed it from one of the guys at work. I thought Brian might get a kick out of trying it."

"Good idea. But I think we better switch to

Dionis Beach. The waves are less intimidating there."

"Would you rather leave it behind and stick with the original plan?"

"No. This is fine." And safer, she added in silence as she moved aside to let him tuck the board into the trunk. There would be a lot more people at Dionis. And as the old saying went, there was safety in numbers. Better yet, the family atmosphere that usually prevailed there would discourage any romantic inclinations.

After securing the board, he stepped back and perused her. "You look too dressed up for the beach."

That was true. Her knee-length wrap skirt and madras print blouse were more suitable for lunch in town. But covering up had helped her feel less exposed—physically and emotionally.

Her spoken response was different, however. "I'm not sure I'll go in the water again until my foot heals."

"Probably wise. But to be honest, I liked the last beach outfit better." He slipped on his sunglasses, hiding his eyes as he gave her that unsettling half-hitch grin.

A typical male reaction, Heather mused, recalling the too-tight T-shirt and too-short shorts she'd had on the day they'd met at Ladies Beach. The kind of reaction that always turned her off.

Yet, much to her annoyance, J.C.'s version caused a little flutter in the pit of her stomach.

The screen door opened, and Brian charged through. Skipping the two steps, he leaped from the porch to the sidewalk, a beach towel slung over his shoulder.

"Hey, J.C."

"Hi, Brian." He turned back to Heather. "Are you ready?"

Considering how her heart was misbehaving, she wished she could say no. But unless she wanted to disappoint Brian, she was stuck. "Yes. Climb in."

Since her nephew was in a talkative mood for once, Heather let her two passengers carry the bulk of the conversation during the short drive. Once at the beach, J.C. and Brian unloaded the trunk as she collected her purse and set the automatic locks.

"Is this yours?" Brian, examining the bodyboard, tossed the question to J.C. as she joined them at the rear of her car.

"No. I borrowed it from a guy at work. Have you ever used one of these?"

"Are you kidding? In St. Louis? All we have is the Mississippi."

"Good point." J.C. grinned. "I'm no expert, but I did try this on a trip to California once. I can give you a few basic instructions. After that you'll be on your own."

Brian took the board and a couple of beach towels, while J.C. picked up the cooler and his own towel, leaving Heather with nothing to carry.

"I can take something," she protested.

J.C. closed the trunk. "I have a better idea. Why don't you hold on to me? It's easy to lose your balance in the deep sand here, even with two good feet." He crooked his elbow. "Shall we?"

He was right again, Heather admitted. And she didn't want to end up facedown on the beach. Yet getting close to J.C. would throw her off balance in a different way.

"Come on, Aunt Heather. I want to try this out."

At Brian's impatient urging, Heather did the logical thing and slipped her hand through J.C.'s arm. Fortunately, he didn't try to initiate a conversation as they traversed the sand. With his biceps bulging beneath her fingers, she doubted she'd have been able to form a single coherent word.

"Is this okay?" J.C. asked after a minute or two.

Jolting to a stop, she evaluated the spot he'd picked, a short distance removed from the family groups and playing children. Close enough to be part of the crowd, but far enough away to give them a little privacy.

"Fine."

A few seconds passed as they stood, unmoving, and she sent him a puzzled look. "What's wrong?"

The corners of his mouth twitched up. "I'll be happy to spread out the towels if you'll give me back my arm."

She was still clinging to him, she realized. Warmth flooded her cheeks, and she jerked her hand away. "Sorry."

"I didn't mind."

She couldn't see his eyes behind his dark glasses. And based on the husky tenor of his voice, she had a feeling that was just as well.

He laid out the towels, then offered her a hand down. "Let me get Brian started with the body-board."

"Good idea." The teen was already at the water's edge, evaluating the surf. "I think he's…"

The words died on her lips as J.C. stripped off his T-shirt in one lithe motion to reveal a broad, powerful chest.

"What were you saying?" He looked down at her as he kicked off his deck shoes.

Heather cleared her throat and tried not to gape. What *had* she been saying? Something about Brian…oh, yeah. "I think he's a pretty good swimmer."

"That's what I want to check out. I'll be back in a few minutes." He tossed his sunglasses onto the towel and took off at a jog toward the water, motioning to Brian to join him as he dived headfirst into the breakers.

Shading her eyes, she watched as J.C. surfaced and waited for Brian before striking out with powerful strokes toward the horizon.

Then she tried to breathe.

She'd gone swimming with Mark plenty of times during their dating days. But never, ever, had she felt such a strong *wow* factor.

It was crazy.

And dangerous.

She had to steel herself against it.

Because as she watched J.C. cut through the swells, she knew it would be very easy to forget about her vow to avoid romance. To forget he was leaving in a few weeks. To forget about the betrayal that seemed to be the fate of the Anderson women.

And with no effort at all, it would be easy to believe this man was special—and worthy of her trust.

Especially when the sun reflecting off J.C.'s wet skin made it shimmer like a suit of armor.

The kid was good, J.C. noted, keeping a close watch on Brian as they aimed toward the horizon. But he wasn't used to ocean swimming, and they were getting into deep water. It was time to turn back.

Yet deep water awaited him on the beach, too, J.C. acknowledged as he switched directions and headed back toward the shore, signaling Brian to do the same.

Slowing his pace to match the teen's, he bought himself a few minutes to plan his strategy. He was the one who'd told Heather a day at the beach wouldn't be a big deal. And he'd meant it. But that had been three days ago. Three days without a glimpse of her. Three days that had felt like an eternity.

A swell lifted J.C., and he rode it out. Fighting a force as powerful as the sea was an exercise in futility and would only wear him out. Kind of like trying to fight his attraction to the charming tearoom owner, he admitted ruefully. He was just going to have to let it dissipate on its own.

Or not.

And the latter was beginning to seem like a far more probable scenario.

But he intended to keep his promise. He wasn't going to push her. If God's plan for his life included the beautiful woman on the beach, he'd have to wait and watch for direction.

Except patience had never been his strong suit.

His hand touched bottom, and the next wave heaved him onto the beach. Standing, he waited for Brian to regain his footing, then launched into a rudimentary lesson on bodyboarding. In less than five minutes, he'd imparted his entire body of knowledge on the subject.

Leaving the teen to experiment on his own, he rejoined Heather, toweling himself dry before dropping to the sand beside her.

"Brian seems to have picked that up quickly," she noted.

Her attention was on her nephew, and J.C. took the opportunity to admire her flawless profile as he agreed. "He's a quick study."

When she turned his way, he reached for his T-shirt—then sucked in a sharp breath as a shaft of pain shot down his arm.

Concern furrowed Heather's brow, and she reached toward him, hesitated, then drew her hand back. "What's wrong?"

Gritting his teeth, he pulled the shirt over his head. "Nothing."

She inspected the angry red scar peeking below the sleeve of the shirt and ignored his change-the-subject cue. "That looks painful."

"Not usually. The swimming today might have taxed it a little."

"Not to mention the painting on Friday."

He gave a stiff shrug. "I'm supposed to use it." Slipping on his sunglasses, he gestured toward Brian. "He's really getting the hang of that."

She spared her nephew no more than a brief glance. "You don't want to talk about it, do you?"

His jaw hardened, and he focused on Brian as the boy worked to gain control over the unruly body-board. "No."

"Why not?"

He bunched some sand in his fist, wishing she'd drop the subject. "It's a long story, Heather."

"I'm not going anywhere. And Brian seems like he'll be occupied for a while." She let a few beats of silence pass. When she resumed speaking, her voice was soft—and caring. "I noticed it the first day at Ladies Beach, too. Was it a line-of-duty injury, J.C.?"

His throat tightened as he gazed at the distant horizon. He hadn't mentioned the shooting incident to anyone since Burke had pressed him into a discussion about it the day after he'd arrived on Nantucket. But maybe he needed to talk about it. Neither the change of scene nor prayer had alleviated the guilt, which continued to cling to him with the tenacity of a Nantucket deer tick. Perhaps by sharing it with someone who was sympathetic, he'd stumble onto some insights that had so far eluded him.

Taking a deep breath, he gave a curt nod. "Yes. I was shot in a drug-ring sting operation that went bad."

"Was anyone else hurt?"

His gut twisted at her gentle question. "Two cops died." The words came out raw and raspy.

For several moments, only the raucous caw of a gull broke the silence.

"I'm so sorry."

Her quiet empathy seeped through his defenses, and he swallowed past the sudden lump in his throat. "Me, too."

"That's why you're here, isn't it? Because you feel guilty you survived and they didn't. And you needed some time to work through that."

Impressed by her insight, he pulled his knees up and rested his forearms on them, gripping one wrist with the other hand. "Partly." He hadn't planned to say anything else, yet all at once he heard more words coming out of his mouth. "But that's not all I feel guilty about."

"What do you mean?"

Why had he said that? J.C. wondered. He never talked about emotional stuff. The counselor in Chicago had tried her best to get him to open up, to share his feelings about the incident. Instead, he'd simply closed up tighter. If a professional had failed to wedge open his heart, why had Heather succeeded?

One look at her gave him his answer. The soft compassion in her hazel eyes reflected genuine, not professional, concern. She'd told him Friday that she liked him a lot. More than she wanted to. And her intent posture, caring demeanor and total focus demonstrated that. While she might be as averse to the notion of romance as he was, she was nevertheless reaching out to him—with the hand of friendship, if nothing else.

As his fingers began to tingle, he loosened his grip on his wrist. And took the plunge into the murky waters of emotion. "It was an ambush. I made a mistake somewhere along the way. Tipped my hand. That's why two people died."

She frowned. "Why do you think that?"

"An internal investigation didn't turn up any leaks. Until the last minute, only a few people knew about my deep-cover assignment or the details of the bust. The ones who did are all longtime cops who know how to keep their mouths shut." A muscle twitched in his cheek. "It had to be my fault. But I've gone over and over everything I did, and I keep coming up blank. It's been eating at me for weeks."

Fingers brushing the sand beside her, Heather focused on the pattern she was creating. "May I ask you a personal question?"

His lips lifted into a mirthless smile. "What do you call the ones you've *been* asking?"

She conceded his point with a shrug. "Different subject, then."

"Okay." He gave her a wary look.

"I saw you with a Bible that day on the beach. So I assume you're religious. How come your faith hasn't helped you get through this?"

The unexpected twist in the conversation threw him. The last thing he'd expected to talk about today was theology. Nor did he consider himself the most articulate spokesperson on matters of faith.

But her question was a good one. And since it suggested she was a seeker, it deserved his full attention.

Doing his best to switch gears, he angled more toward her. "I take it you aren't a believer?"

She shrugged and smoothed out the flawed geometric pattern she'd created in the sand. "No. My mom got religion toward the end of her life and tried to pull me along with her, but to be honest, I was turned off. While she and my dad were married, he handled everything business related...finances, bills, home maintenance. When they separated, she had to learn how to do it all herself. The hard way. As a result, she always preached the gospel of self-reliance. Yet in the end she sold out and put everything in God's hands."

Heather gave him a troubled look. "But she suffered and died, anyway. And your faith doesn't seem to have taken away your anguish over what happened in Chicago."

She'd nailed a key argument of skeptics, and he searched for the words that would help her understand.

"Believing doesn't take away suffering and doubts, Heather. Mother Teresa is a good example. She labored most of her life under terrible conditions to bring love and compassion and hope to the poorest of the poor. She was praised by everyone for her great faith. Yet after she died, her letters revealed a soul in darkness. For most of her life, she felt distanced from God. Surrounded by blackness. But she continued doing what she felt called to do, despite her despair.

"That's what faith is all about. Believing, hoping, trusting even in the darkest hours. I trust the Lord, and I know He'll provide the answers I'm searching for in His time if I put everything in His hands."

"It would be nice to have such a sense of certainty." There was a wistful quality to her words. "But I don't think I could relinquish control of my life to anyone. I'd feel…smothered. Shackled."

"Believe it or not, the opposite happens. It's freeing when God is in charge."

She sifted the sand, watching the grains slip through her fingers. "Have you always believed?"

"Not to the extent I do now. But my mother had a strong faith. And I had a very persistent college buddy who dragged me to services one Sunday after he watched me struggling to keep my family together. That visit got me started on the right road."

A capricious breeze ruffled Heather's hair, and she brushed the silky strands back from her face. "Brian told me Nathan is in prison."

"Yeah." J.C. felt the familiar twinge in the pit of his stomach as he thought about the train wreck that was his brother's life.

"You've had a lot of tough things to deal with for a lot of years."

Compared to her, he supposed that was true. There might be troubled marriages in Heather's background, but there was a lot more bad stuff in his. Yet dwelling on it was an invitation to bitterness.

He lifted one shoulder. "You cope with the hand you're dealt."

"Some do it better than others."

That, too, was true. He'd managed to rise above his past, for the most part. Marci had, too. Nathan was still mired in muck. And perhaps always would be, he thought as a wave of despair washed over him.

It was time to change the subject.

Gesturing toward Brian again, he brought the conversation back to the reason for this outing. "I'd like to think your nephew could learn to do that. He appears to be getting back on track."

To his relief, Heather followed his lead. "I agree. He seems to do better when he's occupied." Shifting into a cross-legged position, she tucked her skirt around her legs. "I wish I knew some good, solid young people his age to introduce him to while he's here. That kind of positive peer influence could be helpful."

An idea took shape in J.C.'s mind. "I have a thought. The church I'm attending here has a high school–age youth group that does service projects during the summer, mixed in with social activities. It's designed to teach kids real-world skills, while instilling a sense of social responsibility. This Wednesday they're going to do some painting for an elderly resident in 'Sconset, with a beach party afterward. If you don't mind the church affiliation, I could invite Brian. I volunteered to help part of the day."

Gratitude warmed her eyes. "That sounds perfect. And we know he's had some experience painting."

"Are you guys talking about me?"

J.C. and Heather turned in unison as the dripping teen bounded up the beach.

"Yes, we were." Heather flipped up the lid of the cooler. "Are you hungry?"

"Starved." He flopped onto his towel as she passed out sandwiches and soft drinks. "Do you have another painting job at the house?"

"No, but J.C. has one."

When Heather looked his way, J.C. took the handoff. "A youth group at the church I'm attending is going to paint a picket fence for a senior citizen this

Wednesday, and I thought you might want to help. You did a great job on your aunt's house."

Brian scrunched up his face. "Church kids are dorks." He took a huge bite of his turkey sandwich.

"Why do you say that?" J.C. snagged a bag of chips and opened the top, keeping his tone conversational.

"My mom's been dragging me to church lately, and she forced me to go to a youth group meeting." He kept chewing as he spoke. "It was the pits."

"Your mom goes to church?"

From Heather's startled question, it was clear this was news to her, J.C. concluded.

"Yeah. And the kids are all losers."

"That might be true there, but the kids at my church are pretty awesome." J.C. spread some mustard on his sandwich. "One of the guys is a fantastic hockey player. A lot of college scouts have come out here to look at him."

"Yeah?" Brian shot J.C. an interested glance.

"And last year one of the girls was a national finalist in the Junior Miss program."

Brian stopped chewing. "That's pretty cool."

"Another guy teaches at one of the island's surfing schools."

Brian swallowed his bite of sandwich and adopted the carefully indifferent, "I'm interested but I still want to appear cool" attitude J.C. often observed in young teens. "So how many kids will be at this painting thing?"

"I think fifteen have signed up. Afterward,

they're going to have a barbecue and play a little beach volleyball. I'll be there part of the time, too. I was going to go out later in the day, but I could make a quick stop in the morning and introduce you to a few of the kids if you want to go."

"I guess that would be okay." Brian took another bite of his sandwich.

Heather stepped back into the conversation and directed her question to J.C. "Are you working nights again this week?"

"Yes."

"When do you sleep?"

He grinned at her. "After I introduce Brian around, I'll come back and crash. I was going to go out again about five and help supervise the wrap-up party. We could use a few more chaperones for that if you could squeeze it in."

Uh-oh. Bad move, J.C. berated himself. Manufacturing reasons to interact with Heather was *not* a good idea.

But maybe she'd follow the prudent path and decline.

No such luck.

"I could help out after the tearoom closes."

"That would be cool, Aunt Heather," Brian chimed in. "What's for dessert?"

She shifted sideways to rummage through the cooler, withdrawing a plate of assorted tea pastries. "These are leftovers from yesterday. I didn't think you guys would mind."

"I'll take these kinds of leftovers any day." Brian helped himself to three different pastries.

When she extended the plate toward him, J.C. took a chocolate tart. "Thanks."

Weighing the tart in his hand, he watched as she selected a miniature éclair for herself and took a bite. A few specks of the custard filling clung to her lips, and J.C. found himself fixated on her mouth.

Oh, brother. This was not good.

Forcing himself to turn away, he popped the whole chocolate tart into his mouth and tried to figure out how the woman beside him had managed to totally disrupt his equilibrium in the space of a few short weeks.

As the rich chocolate dissolved on his tongue, the sudden distinctive tang of peppermint kicked in, taking him off guard. That, in turn, gave way to a hint of spice—cinnamon, perhaps?

The innocent little chocolate tart wasn't quite what it had appeared to be, he reflected. Beneath the surface, a subtle blending of flavors and ingredients had produced a dessert of surprising complexity.

Reminding him of its creator.

And the more he learned about her, the more intrigued—and attracted—he became.

Meaning that for the sake of his heart, he intended to spend the rest of this outing in the water with Brian.

Chapter Eleven

This is a mistake.

As Heather waited beside her garage for J.C., that refrain echoed over and over in her mind—as it had been doing ever since she'd agreed to accompany him to 'Sconset to help chaperone today's youth group beach party.

What had she been thinking?

Now that they'd both acknowledged the spark between them—as well as their mutual aversion to romance—they should be avoiding each other, not seeking out opportunities to spend time together. J.C. shouldn't have invited her to help chaperone. And she shouldn't have accepted.

Meaning this thing between them was strong enough to short-circuit rational behavior.

And that was scary.

"Heather!"

At Edith's summons, Heather tamped down her

panic and moved to the half-moon gate in the privet hedge by her garage. The older woman was standing on the back porch of The Devon Rose, holding Heather's wallet.

"You left this on the counter. Julie found it."

Shaking her head, Heather met her neighbor halfway down the brick walk. "Thanks, Edith." She slid it into her purse.

"A little distracted today, are we?" Edith arched her eyebrows and peered past Heather's shoulder. "Is J.C. here yet?"

"No. He should be along any minute."

"This was a brilliant idea, getting Brian involved with the youth group. I don't know why I didn't think of it."

"It wouldn't have mattered. I doubt anyone but J.C. could have convinced him to give it a try."

"He does have a certain persuasive charm." Her eyes began to twinkle. "Is it working on you yet?"

"Edith!" Heather shushed her. Checking over her own shoulder, she lowered her voice. "He and I discussed this, and we agreed that in light of his short stay, it would be inappropriate to pursue anything romantic."

"Humph." The older woman planted her hands on her hips. "If you ask me, you're being way too analytical."

"Better analytical than disillusioned. Or hurt." Heather resettled the strap of her purse on her shoulder. "Thanks again for stepping in to help Julie with the cleanup today. I couldn't have gone otherwise."

Edith smirked at her. "Why do you think I said yes?" Leaning closer, she winked. "That man is a keeper, Heather. And I'm praying you come to that conclusion before it's too late." With a wave, she headed back to the house.

Huffing out an exasperated breath, Heather retraced her steps to the car—where she found J.C. waiting.

"I was about to come looking for you." He flashed her an easy smile. "We were supposed to meet here, right?"

"Right." She'd set it up that way so Edith wouldn't have a chance to throw out any less-than-subtle innuendos to the pair of them.

Her strategy had half worked.

"Did you get some sleep?" Heather slid into the driver's seat as J.C. held her door.

"Enough." He shut her door, then joined her on the passenger side as she put the car in gear. "Any word from Brian?"

"No. And that's good news. I told him not to use the cell phone unless it was an emergency."

"He hit it off right away with two of the kids. I felt comfortable leaving him. And there are plenty of chaperones. Thanks for letting me use your car to run him out there this morning."

"The thanks are all mine, trust me."

To Heather's relief, J.C. confined the conversation to innocent topics during the seven-mile drive to the east side of the island. Once there, he directed her to a small cottage that backed to the sea. A pristine white picket fence delineated the tiny front yard and extended to the back, where it enclosed the more spacious rear grounds, forming a line of demarcation between sand and grass.

The teens were clustered in small groups, intent on cleanup duties. She spotted Brian rinsing brushes as she pulled up, but he was too interested in talking to a girl with a perky blond ponytail to notice their arrival.

J.C. chuckled. "Why do I have a feeling you won't have any problem getting him to stay involved with this group while he's here?"

She gave him a rueful smile. "Yeah. But now I have other things to worry about."

"No, you don't. These are good kids. I've met most of them. They'll keep him occupied with wholesome activities for the remainder of his stay."

"Thanks to you."

He shook his head. "I had no idea if this would work. But I'm glad it did." He scanned the young people, watching as a wiry, wizened older man with thin, neatly combed gray hair walked among them. "That's the owner, Henry Calhoun. I met him this morning. He won all the kids over immediately with his homemade banana nut bread." The hint of a smile softened his lips.

As Heather watched, the elderly man stopped beside Brian and the girl. Whatever he said had them both laughing before he moved on. "I can't believe that's the same insolent kid who showed up here ten days ago with a huge chip on his shoulder."

"The change is remarkable." His expression grew melancholy. "It's too bad Nathan didn't get involved with a group like this when he was Brian's age. It might have made all the difference."

Heather's heart contracted at the ripple of pain and regret that roughened his words. Without stopping to think, she laid her hand on his.

He went still except for a subtle, sinewy flex in his strong, sun-browned fingers as he looked down, then searched her face.

"I'm sorry about Nathan, J.C. I wish I could help you with him as you've helped me with Brian."

His Adam's apple bobbed, and the color of his eyes deepened from ebony to midnight. Slowly, he lifted his free hand and rested his fingers against her cheek, his touch as light as the whisper of a gentle breeze.

Heather stopped breathing.

"At this point, I don't think anyone but God can help Nathan." His voice came out husky. And not quite steady. "But it means a lot to me that you care."

For several moments his gaze held hers. Then, with obvious reluctance, he removed his fingers and managed a smile. "I guess it's time to put on our chaperone hats. Sit tight. I'll get your door."

As he slid out of the car, lifted a hand in greeting

to Brian, and paused to exchange a few remarks
with Henry, Heather didn't have any choice. The
stiffening seemed to have gone out of her legs.

As well as her resolve.

Because Edith could be right.

J.C. might very well be a keeper.

But if he was, how in the world was she supposed
to reconcile the issues that stood between them?

Playing volleyball hadn't been on J.C.'s agenda
at the teen beach party, but he'd needed to expend
some energy. And keep some distance between
himself and the lovely woman who'd spent a good
part of the waning hours of the afternoon and early
evening chatting with Henry and several of the
other chaperones. Avoiding him—just as he'd been
avoiding her.

And the reason was obvious.

Those two simple touches in the car—one initi-
ated by her, one by him—had jacked up the voltage
on the electricity between them.

But he couldn't dodge her all night.

Stepping out of the game, he waved in one of the
kids on the sidelines to take his place and moved
across the sand toward her.

She was talking to Henry's neighbor now, the
E.R. doctor who'd set up the service project. J.C.
had noticed him at Sunday services. A tall, good-
looking guy. Single, too, according to Edith.

That little fact had never mattered to him. But

now that Heather was giving the man her rapt attention…

Just as a frown darkened his brow, she turned his way. Even from a distance, he could sense her sudden tension.

The doctor apparently did, too. Leaning a bit closer—too close, in J.C.'s opinion—he said a few words, then stepped away.

Good.

Moving in, J.C. tried for a smile. "How about some food?"

"Sure."

"I think it's a limited menu. Hot dogs, chips and cookies were all I saw. Not quite like the gourmet fare at The Devon Rose."

"I like hot dogs." She shoved her hands into the pockets of her jeans. "With lots of relish and mustard."

He grinned. "You don't strike me as a hot-dog kind of woman."

She gave him a steady look. "Don't let the trappings of the tearoom fool you. My personal tastes are pretty simple."

Not certain how to interpret that remark, he motioned toward a large piece of driftwood at the edge of the beach. "Grab us a seat, and I'll get the food."

Without waiting for a reply, he headed for the grill.

As he approached it, his cell phone began to vibrate. Still mulling over the undertones in

Heather's comment, he pulled it off his belt and gave the caller ID a distracted glance.

His step faltered.

It was his sergeant from Chicago.

A surge of adrenaline kicked his pulse into high gear. There would be no reason for Dennis to call—unless there had been a break in the narcotics shooting.

Changing direction, he walked a few yards down the beach and pressed the talk button. "Dennis?"

"Yeah. Sorry to bother you on your leave, J.C. But we've got some news on the setup you guys walked into in the warehouse. I thought you'd want to know. Remember your friend Lenny?"

"Yeah." Lenny Cardosi had been J.C.'s ticket into the narc ring. A carefully cultivated source who'd introduced him to the drug honchos and whose loyalty belonged to the highest bidder. A slimeball who'd sell his soul to the devil for the right price. J.C. had felt in need of a shower after every encounter with the man.

"We picked him up on a fencing charge."

"No surprise there. He was always looking for ways to make a fast buck."

"Yeah. He's a piece of work. Anyway, we did a little probing, since we knew he had connections to the ring. Turns out he was willing to plea-bargain the fencing charge with a little information."

J.C. tightened his grip on the phone. "He knows what went wrong?"

"Yeah. Does the name Dwayne Logan mean anything to you?"

Searching his memory, J.C. came up blank. "No."

"Could be he used an alias in the ring. But he was in deep. Anyway, according to Lenny, he has a friend doing time at Pontiac. He went down to see him once and recognized you. Must have been that quick visit you made three months ago, after your brother had the appendectomy. So he had his friend do a little digging, and the friend found out from your brother that you were a cop. That blew your cover and led to the setup."

As the implications registered, J.C. fought back a sudden wave of nausea.

"I know what you're thinking, J.C.," Dennis said, intercepting his train of thought. "But it's unlikely your brother knew the inmate he talked to had any connection to you."

J.C. wanted to believe that. But he couldn't stifle the doubt that knotted his stomach. Nathan had hated his career choice. Hated his brother's unrelenting efforts to persuade him to reconsider his life choices. Hated his brother, period, perhaps.

His last visit to Pontiac had convinced him of that. After the emergency page from his street supervisor informing him that Nathan had suffered a ruptured appendix, he'd made the drive to the correctional facility in record time. Throughout the long night, when it was touch and go, he'd kept a vigil by his brother's side. And when the danger had passed and Nathan was once more lucid, J.C.'s only reward had been a look of cold defiance before his brother had turned away.

But surely Nathan hadn't betrayed him on purpose. *God, please don't let that be true!* he pleaded. *I can cope with his indifference, his antipathy, even. But if he set me up, if he wanted me to die....*

Drawing a ragged breath, J.C. looked out over the ocean. The unseen sun's slow, steady descent on the other side of the island was darkening the ocean on this side. What unseen events had darkened Nathan's life? he wondered for the thousandth time. And why hadn't he been able to help his brother overcome them? The Lord knew he'd tried. But nothing he'd done had been able to halt his brother's decline into a life of crime. Or reach him since.

"You still there, J.C.?"

Dennis's question pulled him back to the present, and he cleared his throat. "Yeah."

"I know it doesn't bring Jack and Scott back, but I hoped it might ease your mind to know they didn't die because you made a mistake. It was just a rotten coincidence."

And perhaps a deliberate setup by his brother. The agonizing uncertainty was a new torment. "I appreciate the call, Dennis."

"No problem. You finding what you need out there?"

"I'm working on it."

"Well, keep working. We want you back. You're a good detective, and you're missed."

That parting comment was the most praise J.C. had ever heard from his taciturn sergeant, and he appreciated the man's words. But they didn't ease the ache in his heart.

Nothing could, except resolving the new question that clamored for an answer.

Had Nathan set him up on purpose?

But if getting to the bottom of the ambush had been a challenge, finding this answer would be even more difficult.

As he struggled to stem a powerful wave of despair, a sudden jarring burst of teen laughter reminded him he was supposed to be getting some food for himself and Heather. He needed to switch gears. Compartmentalize.

Usually, he managed that without any problem.

But today, as he walked back down the beach, all he could think about was the brother he'd tried so hard to love—and to save—who called a small cell in an Illinois correctional center home.

Something was wrong.

J.C.'s tense posture as he veered off from the food line and put the cell phone to his ear was Heather's first clue. The sudden slump of his broad shoulders near the end of the call was the second. And when he slid the phone back into its holder and turned toward her again, his bleak appearance cinched it.

She watched as he got in line. Exchanged a few

words with the kids and the other chaperones. Picked up some food. But he didn't linger. Once he had their plates in hand, he headed toward her.

From a distance, body language alone had told her J.C. was badly shaken. Now, up close, the tightness in his jaw and the rigid line of his lips provided further evidence of trauma, as did the haggard lines in his face, thrown into stark relief by the setting sun.

"Let me grab a couple of sodas." He handed her a plate, set his on the driftwood log and moved off before she could say a word.

Two minutes later he was back. Leaving a modest distance between them, he sat beside her. "Brian seems to be having fun."

He was going to pretend everything was okay, Heather realized. But the slight tremble in his fingers as he picked up his hot dog betrayed him. And it rattled her. This was a man who had always been solid and steady in difficult situations. Whatever had happened must be bad.

And she couldn't ignore it.

"J.C., what's wrong?"

She watched as he shifted his features into neutral. "What do you mean?"

The transformation in his demeanor from anguished to impassive was remarkable. And accomplished through sheer force of will, she suspected.

Gentling her voice, she leaned toward him. "Look, you don't have to pretend with me. I know you're upset."

A slight frown creased his brow. "I must be slipping. Undercover cops are supposed to be able to keep their emotions in check."

"Maybe you don't feel threatened with me."

His eyes darkened again. "That's not quite true."

Heather's heart skipped a beat. "I'm not talking about…that."

"Yeah. I know." He hesitated, then set his untouched hot dog back on his plate. A hint of emotion seeped through his impassive veneer. "That was my sergeant from Chicago. They found out what went wrong with the drug bust."

The bottom dropped out of her stomach. "Was it… It wasn't your fault, was it?"

"In a roundabout way." He recounted the phone conversation, then raked his fingers through his hair. "Now I know how it happened. What I don't know is if it was an intentional setup."

"Do you think your brother is capable of that kind of malice?"

A bleakness settled over his features. "I'd like to say no. But…I'm not sure anymore."

He set his plate on the log beside him and clasped his hands between his knees. "I never did know what went wrong with him. Why he was always so angry. Brian reminded me of him when he first arrived. But the roots of Nathan's anger went far deeper. He was already getting into minor scrapes with the law before Mom died. They got worse once she was gone. At sixteen, he dropped out of school and pretty much thumbed his nose at me. I wasn't surprised when he got busted for armed robbery."

"That had to be hard…watching your brother go to prison."

"Believe it or not, in a way I was relieved. Once he was locked up, I knew I wouldn't get a call some night asking me to ID a body at the morgue." He studied his clenched knuckles, easing the grip that had whitened them.

"Even after he was in prison, I didn't give up on him. In the beginning, I drove down to Pontiac twice a month. Sometimes he'd see me. Most times he wouldn't. After he refused to come to the visitors' room six months in a row, I started writing to him every week instead. I still do. But I never get a response. He's completely shut me out. And I have no idea how to reach him."

His voice choked on the last word, and he bowed his head.

Touching wasn't good. Heather knew that after today's experience in the car. But there was no way she could ignore this strong, decent, caring man's desperate need for consolation.

Setting her soda aside, she scooted closer to J.C. and entwined her fingers with his. "What did your sergeant say?"

He gripped her hand. Hard. "He thinks it was a coincidence. That Nathan has no idea the inmate he talked to had any connection to me."

"He could be right."

"He could also be wrong." The desolation in his eyes ripped at her soul. "Marci gave up on Nathan years ago. Maybe it's time I did, too."

Heather shook her head. "I don't think you're the type to give up on someone you love."

The quiet words hung between them, backed by the steady, predictable rhythm of the surf.

His gaze locked on hers. "I'm not."

She had a feeling they weren't talking about Nathan anymore.

"Hey, Aunt Heather, Erin invited me to come to church on Sunday. Could we go?"

As Brian skidded to a stop in front of them, J.C. released her hand. A chill settled over her fingers, and she had to fight the urge to once again seek out the warmth of his touch.

Trying to refocus, she considered Brian's request. She hadn't been inside a church since her mother's funeral. But she supposed attending the service would be good for Brian. And she doubted Susan would mind.

"Let me check with your mom."

"She'll be cool."

"I'll be there, too," J.C. offered.

"Awesome! You could ride with us. Aunt Heather, some of the guys are going surfing tomorrow at Cisco Beach. Is it okay if I go, too? Jason has an extra board, and he said he'd teach me."

She deferred to J.C. He knew these kids better than she did. "What do you think?"

"Jason's a good kid. I've talked to him quite a bit. He wants to go into law enforcement."

"Are any parents going to be there?" Heather asked Brian.

"Yeah. One of the guy's moms."

"Okay. That works. And now we need to head home." Things were winding down around them, and she still had to add the finishing touches to one of tomorrow's desserts.

The ride back was notable for Brian's enthusiasm and J.C.'s quietness. As he focused on the rapidly falling darkness outside his window, Heather did her best to keep her nephew engaged in conversation.

And she also found herself sending a rare prayer heavenward, asking the Lord to dispel the dark despair from J.C.'s soul.

"Susan? Am I catching you at a bad time?" Heather balanced the phone against her shoulder as she slid a tray of scones into the oven the next morning.

"No. I just came out of a meeting. I was going to call you in a little while, anyway. How's everything going?"

"Much better." Heather had been giving her sister daily reports, so Susan was up to speed on her son's progress. "The outing with the church group went well. He's off surfing today with a bunch of the kids he met. And get this. He wants to go to the service this Sunday."

"Wow! I've been trying to get him interested in doing that for weeks."

"So I heard. When did you start attending church, anyway?"

"About three months ago. I have a good friend who's been urging me to give it a try. Believe it or not, I like it. And it's helped me get through some bad stuff recently."

A niggle of unease put Heather on alert. She was pretty certain her sister wasn't talking about Brian's problems. Or Peter's infidelity. Or even her sprained ankle. "New stuff?"

"Yes." There was a hint of tears in Susan's voice. "Heather, I know Dad is an off-limits subject, but I need to tell you this. He was just diagnosed with a brain tumor."

Brain tumor.

The ominous words echoed in Heather's mind as she struggled to process Susan's bombshell. She'd thought she was past caring what happened to her father, but she was shocked to discover that the news shook her at some deep, elemental level.

"How bad is it?" The question was out before she could stop it.

"It's the size of a small orange."

Another jolt rocked her.

"The good news is the surgeon thinks it's a meningioma. Those usually aren't malignant. And it appears to be pretty accessible on the MRI. But it's still brain surgery." Susan paused. "Here's the thing,

Heather. He'd like to come visit you before the surgery."

"No." Her response was instinctive. And immediate. "I don't want to see him."

"Please, Heather. At least hear him out."

"Why? Nothing can change the fact that he destroyed our family."

"Did he?"

Heather frowned. "What's that supposed to mean?"

"If Mom had forgiven him, maybe we could have all stayed together."

"But he cheated on her! Betrayed her! Broke his marriage vows! How could you expect her to trust him again?"

"I'm not condoning what he did, Heather. He made a big mistake. A combination of poor judgment, too much alcohol and the aftereffects of a fight with Mom."

Heather stepped over to the window above the sink, seeking out the peace and symmetry of her garden. "That doesn't excuse him."

"No. But it was one slip. And he's never stopped regretting it. He tried to make amends, but you know how stubborn Mom could be. I loved her as much as you did, but once she made up her mind on an issue, that was it. And she had a lot of pride. She closed the door with Dad and never looked back."

This was not a discussion Heather wanted to have. When a line had been drawn in the sand, she'd joined her mother, while Susan had managed to keep one foot on both sides. At this late stage, it would feel disloyal to modify her allegiance.

Besides, she knew—better than Susan—how her mother had struggled to build a new life. All because she'd put her hopes and dreams into the hands of a man she'd trusted. A man she'd believed would take care of her and love her all the days of her life.

A man who had failed her.

"Mom got hurt very badly, Susan. I'm not going to judge her after all these years."

"I don't want to be judgmental, either. I'm just trying to get you to recognize there are two sides to this story. And you've never heard Dad's."

As the conversation grew more heated, the wisdom of their decision to make their father a taboo topic was reinforced for Heather. Even this short discussion had created an uncomfortable tension between them.

When the silence lengthened, her sister sighed. "Dad's never stopped loving you, you know."

Heather felt the pressure of tears in her throat. Swallowed past it. "Look, I have to run. I've got a full house today, and I need to do some more baking. How do you want to handle telling Brian about this?"

"I'll call him tonight. And I'll keep praying you change your mind."

As the line went dead and Heather dropped the

phone back into its cradle, Susan's last comment reminded her again of the ill-advised prayer *she'd* offered not long ago, asking the Lord to give her something to think about besides J.C.

What was it Oscar Wilde had written? Something to the effect that when the gods want to punish us, they answer our prayers?

Maybe everything that had happened in the past few weeks to upset her life was one big cosmic joke, Heather mused.

But if it was, she wasn't laughing.

And to make matters worse, she had a sinking feeling the joke wasn't over yet.

As promised, Susan called again that night to give Brian the news about his grandfather.

He didn't take it well.

Heather heard him slam the back door as she was trying, with very little success, to focus on her business expenses spreadsheet. She'd been tense and distracted since getting the news, too.

Closing the document, she went in search of her nephew. She found him in the garden, by the birdbath, hands shoved in pockets, face mutinous in profile. Looking like he was ready to kick something again.

"Is this one of those times you might need a hug?"

At her quiet question, he turned toward her. "That won't make Grandpa better."

"No. But it might help us feel better."

He swiped his sleeve across his eyes. "You don't even care about him."

"I care about you. And we've talked about why your grandfather and I went our separate ways."

"But he loves you!" Brian shoved his hands into his pockets and faced her. "Did you know he carries an old picture of you in his wallet? I saw it last year, when he was buying me a candy bar. It's all yellow and beat-up around the edges."

Heather's heart did a quickstep. Was it possible her father continued to keep her picture with him? After twenty years?

"And he's told me a lot of stories about when you and Mom were little. How you used to go down to the riverfront to watch the fireworks under the Arch on the Fourth of July. How he used to fix your dolls and your bicycles and even a dancing shoe once, right before your recital, at his tool bench in the garage. How you used to take picnics to Hawn State Park in the fall and hike along Pickle Creek."

Thrown off balance by a sudden rush of memories, Heather sank onto the wooden bench beside her.

"Don't you remember any of that, Aunt Heather?"

"Yes." She cleared her throat to dispel the hoarseness. "We had a good life. That's why it hurt so much when your grandfather destroyed it."

"But it's not too late to rebuild some of it. He's a really good guy."

"Too many years have gone by, Brian."

"Mom says it's never too late to try to fix problems."

As he sank down on the other end of the bench, a cardinal settled on the birdbath. The concrete bowl was dry, Heather noted. A lapse on her part, thanks to all the upheaval in her life in recent weeks. She needed to replenish it.

And perhaps she needed to replenish her well of compassion, too.

Jolted by that radical thought, she tried to dismiss it. Tried to tell herself she had justifiable reasons for the choices she'd made about her father.

But J.C. could have said the same thing about his relationship with his brother, her conscience reminded her. *Yet in spite of all Nathan has done to disrupt his life, he's never written him off or shut him out.*

Heather couldn't refute the truth of that. And it was also a pretty powerful witness to the principles that guided J.C.'s life. He might not talk much about his faith unless prompted. But he lived its key tenets.

"I'm sorry if I upset you, Aunt Heather. I just feel real bad about Grandpa."

At Brian's subdued comment, she turned to him. "It's okay. I know how hard it is when someone you love gets sick. That's how I felt about your grandma."

"She was a cool lady."

"Yes, she was." Heather's voice scraped on the last word.

"Do you think I could have that hug now?"

"You bet."

But as Brian wrapped her in his skinny adolescent arms, Heather knew she needed the comfort more than he did.

Chapter Twelve

"Happy early Fourth of July to my favorite sister."

A groggy groan greeted J.C.'s salutation. "What time is it?"

"Nine-thirty."

"It's only eight-thirty in Chicago. Call me back in a couple of hours."

"No can do. I'm going to church. And I've got other commitments later." J.C. picked up a mug of coffee from the counter in the tiny kitchenette of his cottage. "Did you work late?"

"Yeah." Marci stifled a yawn. "And I have to be back at eleven."

"I thought you were going to relax a little this summer. What's with all the long hours?"

"Bills, big brother. Bills."

"Do you have some unusual expenses?" He kept his tone conversational, knowing he was treading on delicate ground. Even when she was in dire straits, she never took a dime from him. Instead, she worked longer hours waitressing at Ronnie's Diner—a dive with a questionable clientele. As far as he was concerned, she was too independent for her own good. An opinion she did *not* share.

"The rent on my apartment is going up in August." She yawned again. "I want to stockpile some funds to cover it before school starts. And they're hiking up the tuition again this year, too. So what's up with you?"

Her message was clear: the subject of her finances was closed.

"I do have some news. My sergeant called on Thursday. They found out why the bust went bad."

"What happened?" The last vestiges of sleep vanished from her voice.

"Someone connected with the drug ring spotted me at Pontiac when Nathan had appendicitis."

"Another inmate?"

"No. A visitor."

"How did he know you were a cop?"

"He asked the guy he came to see to grill Nathan about me."

Several beats of silence ticked by as she arrived at the conclusion he was trying to dismiss.

"Nathan set you up."

"My sergeant doesn't think so. He doubts Nathan knew why the guy was asking about me."

"But he could have." Marci's words simmered with anger.

J.C. took another swig of coffee. The brew tasted bitter against his tongue, and he set it aside. "It's a huge leap from alienation to malice, Marci. I choose not to believe it was intentional."

"You need to write him off, J.C." Frustration nipped at her words. "I know you want to keep your promise to Mom, but you've gone above and beyond. She wouldn't expect the impossible."

"Nothing's impossible with God."

"This would take a miracle."

"Those can happen." J.C. checked his watch. "Listen, I have to run. I'm hitching a ride to church, and I don't want to keep her waiting."

Whoops. Big mistake, he realized.

"You're riding to church with a woman?"

There was no way out now. "Yeah. And her nephew. She runs the tearoom next door."

"Is she single?"

"I didn't come here for romance, Marci."

"So she's available? Cool!"

"Don't push on this unless you want me to reciprocate."

He knew that would end the discussion. His sister was as bristly as a porcupine whenever he asked about *her* social life. As far as he could tell, she didn't have one. And he hadn't a clue why. Not only did she have blond good looks and a centerfold figure, she was smart and funny. But whenever the topic arose, she closed up tight as a Nantucket clam.

True to form, she changed the subject. "Fine. I

wouldn't want you to be late for church, anyway. Listen—say a prayer for me if you think about it, okay?"

The hint of wistfulness in her request took him off guard.

"I always do. And I'll call you again next week."

"I know. You always were the dependable type." There was silence for a second, and when she continued, a tremor ran through her words. "Look, I don't want to get mushy or anything, but…you're a good guy, J.C. Thanks for sticking with me."

As they hung up, Marci's words warmed him.

But whether it was wise or not, he couldn't help wishing a certain tearoom owner shared his sister's sentiment.

Heather felt like a fraud.

As she and J.C. entered the small church, Brian a step behind them, it seemed as if every head turned in their direction. Most of the faces were unfamiliar. But she did spot Julie and Todd. Kate and Craig from next door were there, too. Although Maddie and Vicki, their two children, grinned and waved, all four of the adult demeanors registered surprise.

But no one appeared more taken aback than Edith.

The older woman's eyes widened and her mouth dropped open as she caught sight of them. Leaning close to Chester, she whispered in his ear. A moment later the older man twisted their way, his welcoming grin and wink easing some of the tension in Heather's shoulders.

If J.C. was aware of the interested glances their entrance was attracting, he ignored them. Ushering her into a pew about halfway back on the opposite side from Edith, he sat beside her.

Despite his reassuring smile, Heather still felt like a phony. How in the world had she allowed herself to be talked into this? Even her beloved mother had only managed to persuade her to attend services twice.

But since she was here, she supposed she might as well approach it with an open mind.

The music was pleasant, she decided. In place of booming hymns pounded out on an organ, expressive piano renderings filled the modest chapel. And the Bible passages read by a kind-faced middle-aged minister were thought provoking.

But much to her surprise, it was the Fourth of July–themed sermon that gripped her. Especially the conclusion.

"As you know, we live in a country that was founded and has flourished on the principles of self-reliance and freedom," the minister told the congregation. "A nation where individual rights are respected and protected. Yet despite our firm belief in independence and personal freedom, our country couldn't function without laws. Imagine New York City or Chicago without traffic regulations."

He leaned forward, his posture earnest. "I doubt

any of us would advocate doing away with civil laws. Yet how often we chafe against God's laws—the ones that prevent traffic jams in our souls and preserve order in our spiritual lives. My friends, those laws don't restrict or confine us. They set us free to journey on the path we were meant to travel. Can you imagine what a wonderful world this would be if we followed God's laws and embraced the principles of love, charity and forgiveness? If we let go of old grudges and opened ourselves to new life?

"This week, as we celebrate the birthday of our country and the freedoms it protects, I'd like to suggest that you give yourselves a present—the spiritual freedom that comes from following the laws our Lord gave us. Put your trust in them—and in Him. Because only by doing that do we find the lasting peace and serenity and order that offer us true freedom."

As the service continued, Heather mulled over the man's words. For years she'd avoided relying on anything or anyone. Especially religion, with the attendant rules she viewed as confining and controlling. Yet the minister's comments resonated with her. She understood the need for order. That was why she had standard operating procedures for her business—and her life. Those self-imposed rules stabilized her world and allowed her to work more efficiently.

Might faith provide a similar framework on a

spiritual level? Help her put some order into those aspects of her life where she was floundering?

That notion held a certain appeal.

Yet faith required trust. And forgiveness. Two major stumbling blocks for her.

It was a dilemma she had no idea how to resolve.

Fifteen minutes later, as the closing notes of the final hymn died away, she was still struggling with that quandary as J.C. leaned toward her.

"Well…what did you think?"

She turned toward him. Attired today in a subtly patterned sport jacket that emphasized the breadth of his shoulders, a cream-colored shirt, and beige slacks that hinted at his muscular legs, he oozed magnetism. It was no wonder every woman in the church seemed to be looking at him.

"The sermon was interesting."

"Aunt Heather, could we go to Downyflake? Everyone hangs out there after church." Brian dropped into step behind them as they exited the pew.

"Sure. Unless J.C. needs to get home."

"Nope. A sugar doughnut from The Flake sounds perfect."

Perfect.

The word echoed in her mind as J.C. took her arm while they descended the front steps of the church.

Because that was how it felt when she was by his side.

* * *

Two days later, when the doorbell rang at The Devon Rose, Heather pulled off her baking mitts and checked the clock. J.C. was a little early, but that was okay. She hadn't seen much of him since Sunday, thanks to his longer-than-usual holiday hours. And she'd missed him.

That was why she'd jumped at his offer to pick up Brian from today's youth group outing. With a private holiday-eve tea booked for this afternoon—and neither Edith nor Julie available to help—it was going to be crazy.

Brushing a spattering of flour off her denim-clad leg, she headed for the hall. It was odd that J.C. had come to the front door, but perhaps he was on his way back from an errand.

Trying to suppress an anticipatory surge of adrenaline, she took a calming breath, smiled, pulled open the door…and froze.

"Hello, Heather."

As she stared at the older man on her doorstep, a rushing sound filled her ears, rocking her world. Although white hair had replaced brown, the once-smooth brow had become creased by two decades of living, and the broad shoulders she remembered had rounded, she'd recognize her father's voice anywhere.

Her fingers twitched on the door as her instincts screamed at her to slam it in his face.

As if sensing her intent, Walter Anderson wrapped

one hand around the door frame, his expression pleading. "Please, Heather. Give me five minutes."

Panic numbed her. She couldn't shut the door without mashing his fingers. But she didn't have to talk to him. She *wouldn't* talk to him.

Backing up, she edged the door to within inches of his knuckles. "I have nothing to say to you." Strain choked her voice.

"You don't have to say anything. Just listen. Please. I came a long way to see you."

"You wasted your time."

A spasm of pain writhed across his face. "I can't leave without talking to you."

"Then you'll be here a long time." Heather tightened her grip on the edge of the door.

A faint knock echoed behind her, and she grasped that excuse to end the encounter. "There's someone at my back door. I have to go."

Her father hesitated. Dropped his hand and withdrew a slip of paper from his pocket. Held it out. "This is my cell phone number if you change your mind. Please take it."

She looked down at the paper in his unsteady fingers. In the background, the dustiness of his shoes registered on some peripheral level. That wasn't like him. Walter Anderson had always been a stickler about polished shoes. And these had clocked a lot of miles. She could see they were worn at the edges. He must have…

Another knock sounded at the rear of the house, and she retreated a step, ignoring the paper.

As she pushed the door closed, she took one last look at him.

And was sorry she had.

Tears were welling in his eyes.

A shock wave rippled through her. No matter what blow life had dealt, her father had always remained in control. He'd been the kind of invincible man a daughter could look up to. The kind she could trust to take care of her. To make things right when everything went wrong. To solve her problems.

But in the end, Walter Anderson had turned out to be the biggest problem of all.

And it appeared she'd been wrong about the strong part, too. Or maybe life after the divorce had beaten him down. The weary slump of his shoulders, the deep-seated fatigue in his eyes, the physique bordering on gaunt suggested life hadn't been easy for the man she'd once idolized.

But that wasn't her problem, she reminded herself, doing her best to snuff out the compassion her father's tears had kindled. He'd created his own problems.

Turning away, she shut the door.

And started to shake.

Another knock sounded on the back door, this one more forceful.

J.C.

Willing her trembling legs to carry her forward, she stumbled through the house and opened the back door.

"Hi. I was beginning to think…" J.C.'s smile of greeting evaporated. "What's wrong?"

Her breath hitched. "My father just sh-showed up at my front door."

Taking her arm, he gently guided her to the kitchen table and urged her into a seat. Then he sat beside her and reached for her hand, entwining her fingers with his.

"Just sit for a minute and take a few deep breaths."

Heather closed her eyes and did as he instructed, drawing comfort from his steady, warm clasp.

After a few minutes, he reached over and brushed some stray strands of hair back from her forehead. "Would you like a cup of tea?"

As she looked into his tender, caring eyes, it took every ounce of her willpower to fight the yearning to take shelter in his strong arms. "Yes."

She started to rise, but he pressed her back into her seat with a firm hand on her shoulder. "I may be a coffee drinker, but I can manage to make a cup of tea." He flashed her a quick smile. "What kind would you like?"

"Chamomile. There are some bags in the drawer to the right of the sink."

Three minutes later, he set a steaming cup in front of her. She took a slow sip as he reclaimed his seat.

"Any idea what prompted this?"

"Yes." She recounted the information Susan had passed on about the brain tumor.

"So he came all this way in that condition just to talk to you?"

A subtle nuance in his tone put her on the defensive. "I told Susan I didn't want to see him. I know she passed that on." She fiddled with her cup, not liking her strident tone. And feeling more off balance by the minute. "Do you think I was…that it was wrong to send him away?"

He lifted one shoulder. "It's your decision, Heather. But you know how your mother wanted to get right with the Lord before she died? It could be your father wants to get right with you."

"It's a little late for that."

"Are you sure?"

Propping her elbow on the table, she dipped her chin and massaged her forehead, where a dull ache had begun to throb. "I used to be. Now…I don't know. But even thinking about getting back together with my dad somehow seems disloyal to my mom."

"Did she encourage the rift?"

"No. She never spoke badly about him to me. And she never discouraged me from talking to him when he called, or suggested I ignore his letters. It was my choice. It was the only tool I had to punish him for what he'd done to our family."

"What exactly did he do?"

At his quiet question, Heather wrapped her hands around her cup, letting the heat warm her cold fingers. "He had a fling with his high school sweetheart the night of their class reunion. According to Susan, he drank too much at the event."

"Did he drink a lot as a rule?"

"No. I can't ever remember him having so much as a glass of wine."

"Where was your mom?"

"Susan says he and Mom had a fight that day, and she stayed home."

"Sounds like a lot of things went wrong all at one time."

"That's no excuse for infidelity."

"I agree." J.C. folded his hands on the table. "How did your mom find out about this?"

"A friend of hers had been at the reunion, and when she went back to her hotel, she saw him go into the woman's room. She called my mother, and Mom went over to check things out herself. Marched right up and knocked on the door. My dad was in there."

"And that was the end of the marriage?"

She thought she detected a hint of recrimination in his tone, and her anger flared. "Of course! Would you expect her to hang around with a man who didn't respect or love her enough to honor his marriage vows? How would she ever have held her head up again in front of her friends?"

"Is that what it was all about, then? Pride?"

"No! It was about infidelity. And betrayal. And shattered trust." She shook her head and expelled a bitter, resigned breath. "All the things that seem to be the legacy of the Anderson women."

A few beats of silence ticked by as J.C. rested his elbows on the table and steepled his fingers. "I think I just figured out why you've steered clear of relationships," he said softly.

She gave a short, mirthless laugh. "Do you blame me? My father, my brother-in-law, the one guy I was serious about—they all cheated. What does that say about the judgment of the Anderson women?"

"I have confidence in the judgment of one of them."

Her throat tightened. "I don't. And I'm not up for that discussion today. I have to decide what to do about my father."

Compassion softened the strong planes of his face. "You could try forgiveness, like Reverend Kaizer talked about last Sunday."

Heather shook her head. "That sounds good in theory. But all that turn-the-other-cheek stuff can leave a person pretty beat-up."

"Forgiveness isn't about putting yourself back in the line of fire. It's about letting go of bitterness and blame. And it can be very freeing to the forgiver as well as the forgiven." He leaned forward, searching her eyes. "Was your father sorry, Heather?"

At his question, an image of the final scene from that long-ago night replayed in her mind. Her father had returned not long after her mother. Susan had been away at college, starting her freshman year, and her mother had sent Heather to her room to pack for a weekend visit to her grandparents' house while her parents sorted through "the situation," as her mother had referred to it.

Instead, she'd cracked her door and tried to listen to the conversation taking place in her parents' room, her stomach in knots. But no voices had been raised in the closed-door discussion.

When her father had emerged, however, the gray cast to his skin had shocked her. He'd spotted her in her doorway, and his features had twisted in anguish as he'd walked toward her. But she'd slammed the door, sliding the bolt in place as tears streamed down her cheeks. Though he'd begged her to talk to him, though his remorse had been clear, she'd ignored his pleas. And when she'd returned from her weekend, he'd been gone.

"Being sorry didn't change anything, J.C." She gripped her cup and blinked away the moisture blurring her vision. "His mistake destroyed our family. For months afterward, I felt like someone had died."

Once again, J.C. reached over and took her hand, caressing it with soothing strokes of his thumb. "At least you have the opportunity for a second chance."

She knew he was thinking of Nathan. The brother who'd ignored his repeated attempts to make contact…just as she had ignored her father's diligent efforts to connect in the early years.

And would perhaps ignore them now.

She also knew what J.C. would do in her place.

"May I ask you one more question?"

His careful tone put her on alert, and she tensed. "I guess so."

"What would your father have to do to earn your forgiveness?"

"Fix what he broke. But it's too late for that."

"So are you saying that no matter how sincere his remorse, no matter how deep his contrition, you'd never be able to forgive him?"

Heather shifted in her chair. If she said yes, she'd sound hard-hearted and uncharitable. And she wasn't that way.

Except maybe with her father.

"I don't expect you to answer that for me, Heather." J.C.'s words were gentle, and there was no reproach, no judgment, in his eyes. "But it might be good if you answer it for yourself. Is there a Bible anywhere in the house?"

"My Mom had one. It's still in her room."

"Check out Ephesians four, verses thirty-one and thirty-two. It might help." J.C. looked at his watch. "I better get Brian, or he'll think we forgot him. Will you be okay?"

"Yes."

With one final squeeze of her hand, J.C. released it and pushed through the back door.

As quiet descended once more in her kitchen, Heather gave herself five more minutes to sip her tea and try to settle her nerves before she called Susan and got back to work.

When at last she rose to rinse her cup in the sink, she did feel better.

But while the tea had contributed to her calmer state, she also knew the caring, dark-eyed cop who lived next door could claim most of the credit.

Chapter Thirteen

"Dad's on Nantucket?"

Susan's shocked question echoed over the line, confirming Heather's suspicion that her sister hadn't known about their father's trip.

"Yes. He showed up at my door this afternoon." Heather began arranging the three-tiered servers in a neat, precise line on the counter.

Her sister blew out a frustrated breath. "He told me he was going on retreat for a few days. Said he needed to make his peace with a few things. He's been in touch by cell, like he promised…but I never suspected he was planning a trip like this. And he shouldn't be traveling in his condition. Is he okay?"

"He seemed fine. I'm putting you on speaker. I've got a special tea this afternoon, and I need to keep moving." She set the phone on the counter and began filling small serving dishes with strawberry preserves.

"I can't imagine how he managed this. Physically or financially."

"Dad always made good money. I doubt he's hurting for cash."

"Oh, Heather." Susan's sigh came over the line. "Dad left his job a month after he and Mom split."

She stopped spooning out the preserves. That was news. She'd assumed he'd stayed in his stable, if unexciting, position as an actuary with an insurance company until he'd retired. It wasn't a job that would ever have brought him wealth, but it would have provided security and a steady income.

"Why did he quit?"

"He'd been wanting to for a long time. That was why he and Mom fought the day of the reunion. Why there was a strain in their marriage."

Heather frowned. "I never picked up any strain between them."

"I didn't, either, until a year before the split. Mom and Dad were good at maintaining a placid front."

She supposed that was true. Even on the night of the reunion, despite the emotional turmoil her parents must have been experiencing, there had been no raised voices.

"What did he do instead?" Heather finished the preserves and moved on to the clotted cream.

"Opened a bookstore. He always wanted to, but Mom thought it was too risky. She liked the assurance of a steady paycheck. And the start-up costs would have put them into debt. She was worried about college tuition and paying off the house and cars."

"In other words, she was being practical."

"I'm not criticizing Mom, Heather. I'm explaining the situation."

"How do you know all this, anyway?" A flare of annoyance sharpened her words.

"I overheard. I observed. I asked Dad. I asked Mom, too, but she would never talk about it. You know how stubborn she could be. And security conscious."

"She had reason to be. Especially after she and Dad split."

"She was like that before, too."

Heather ignored that. "Does Dad still have the bookstore?"

"No. It was never a big moneymaker. And, in the end, the growth of chains was the death knell for a lot of independent bookstores. He had to close three years ago."

"So it wasn't such a good idea, after all." Meaning her mother's concerns had been valid.

"I don't think he has a single regret. About that, anyway. He told me once he'd felt as if he'd been in prison working at the insurance company, but that the bookstore set him free. Why don't you ask him about it yourself?" When silence met her question, Susan spoke again. "You *are* going to talk to him, aren't you?"

"I don't know."

"Come on, Heather. Let the past go. Dad's a good man. He always has been. He just isn't perfect. But who is?"

A tall, dark and handsome cop came to mind, but Heather pushed that dangerous thought aside. Susan was right. No one was perfect—including J.C. To believe otherwise was a recipe for disaster.

"I'll think about it, Susan. That's the best I can promise."

"I guess that will have to do. Call me if anything else develops, okay?"

Promising she would, Heather ended the call and picked up a plate of scones, giving each a final critical inspection before placing it on a tiered server. She set aside those that weren't perfect.

Like you set your father aside.

At the rebuke from her conscience, Heather paused. Everything seemed to be pushing her toward a reconciliation. And perhaps she did need to consider it, she conceded. When she'd decided to cut off her father, she'd been an adolescent as strong-willed and angry as the Brian who'd arrived on Nantucket almost three weeks ago. But two decades had passed. Her grudge was twenty years old.

Maybe it was time to let it go.

A series of beeps reminded her to check on a batch of mini-quiches. For the rest of today and tomorrow, the holiday crowds wouldn't leave her a minute to call her own.

But after that, she had a lot of thinking to do. And a life-changing decision to make.

"Yoo-hoo. Anybody home?"

At Edith's greeting, Heather turned from the stainless-steel prep table in the center of her kitchen, where she was decorating a tray of dark chocolate tarts with milk chocolate curls. Her neighbor stood on the other side of her screen door, holding a plate of brownies with small American flags stuck in the middle.

The sweet treat was a dead giveaway. The Lighthouse Lane matchmaker was here to get the scoop on Heather's visit to church Sunday with J.C.

"Come in, Edith."

Too late. The older woman was already through the door and halfway across the room. Sliding the plate of brownies onto the counter, she smoothed her red knit top over her white capris. A royal blue scarf around her neck rounded out her patriotic attire.

"In honor of the holiday." She gestured toward the brownies. "Not that they can compare to your baking, of course. But teenagers like them. Are you going to the fireworks tonight?"

"Brian is. With a group of kids from the church. I'll be baking."

"I thought you and J.C. might pair up for the festivities."

"He's working the event." Heather knew where

Edith was heading and decided diversionary tactics were in order. "Guess who showed up here yesterday? My father."

Edith's face went blank. "Your father is on Nantucket?"

"Yes. He has a brain tumor and wants to reconnect."

Edith's mouth gaped open, and she slid onto a stool at the counter, abandoning her original mission. "Okay. Start at the beginning."

Heather filled her in, working as she talked. "I called Susan after he left," she concluded. "And I learned a few unsettling things about my parents' marriage."

Propping her elbow on the counter, Edith tapped her index finger against her lips, as if weighing her words. "Your mom and dad did have some problems even before your dad strayed."

Now it was Heather's turn to be surprised. Her mother had never, ever talked to anyone about the reason behind her divorce. "You knew about that?"

"Not until a few weeks before your mom died. After she found the Lord, she began to struggle with a lot of issues, and I guess she needed a sympathetic ear. She was working through them, but I think she expected to have more time."

The swiftness of her demise had taken everyone by surprise, Heather acknowledged. Instead of the eight or nine months the doctors had predicted, she'd been gone in sixteen weeks.

"Here's the thing, Heather." Edith leaned forward, her expression sober. "I got the feeling your mother was having some regrets about how she handled the whole situation with your father. Not just the infidelity episode, but other things that had caused dissension in their marriage. She didn't go into a lot of detail, but I know some of it had to do with your dad's job."

"Edith? You about ready?"

At Chester's summons, Edith checked her watch. "I'll be right there," she called over her shoulder. Sliding off the stool, she leaned over to pat Heather's hand. "If you want my opinion, I think she was carrying around a boatload of guilt for not encouraging you to maintain some ties with your father, as your sister did. My guess is she'd want you to talk to him." Moving toward the door, Edith stopped on the threshold. "By the way, did you discuss this with J.C.?"

"Yes."

"What did he say?"

The perfectly formed chocolate curl in Heather's hand melted into a gooey blob, and she reached for a dishcloth to wipe off the mess. "Pretty much the same thing you did."

"Good man." Edith gave a satisfied nod and pushed through the door. It banged shut behind her.

Somehow Heather managed to keep most of her disturbing thoughts at bay during the hectic day. But they surfaced again as she climbed the stairs to her bedroom and caught a glimpse of the distant fireworks through her window. A dazzling burst of white rained shooting stars over Nantucket Harbor, creating a momentary illusion of magic.

Was it possible she'd been living all these years with a different kind of illusion? she wondered.

Had she wrongly put the blame for the disintegration of her family solely on her father?

Should she take the leap and listen to what he had to say?

Or was it too late to try to rebuild that relationship?

Heather didn't know the answer to those questions. And one trip to church hadn't given her the kind of connection with the Lord that J.C. relied upon.

But she could sure use some divine guidance about now.

J.C.'s radio crackled to life, and he pulled it off his belt. Yesterday's holiday festivities were over, but a celebratory atmosphere remained among the throng of visitors. He'd been pulled from one incident to another since the beginning of his shift—which had already been extended by several hours, thanks to a family emergency that had delayed his replacement. He was more than ready to call it a day.

"FP four, go."

"FP four, please respond to the corner of Federal and Pearl for a report of a man falling on the sidewalk. Unknown problem. NFD is en route also."

"FP four, received." Clipping the radio back on his belt, J.C. picked up his pace.

As he approached the accident scene two minutes later, the small cluster of people eased back, revealing a white-haired man sitting on the sidewalk, his back against a planter. He seemed a little pale, but a quick scan didn't reveal any obvious injuries. J.C. dropped to the balls of his feet beside him.

"Sir, I'm Officer Clay. We have EMTs on the way."

"I don't need medical assistance. I just want to sit for a few minutes."

Looking up, J.C. addressed the group that had gathered around. "Did any of you see what happened?"

"Yes." A stout middle-aged woman stepped forward. "He was walking along and began to sway. Next thing I knew, he'd fallen."

"Was he unconscious?"

"No, young man, I wasn't." At the white-haired man's firm reply, J.C. redirected his attention to the victim. "And I'm perfectly lucid. You can ask me any questions you like. After you help me over to that bench and this crowd disperses."

Without waiting for J.C. to respond, the man grasped the edge of the planter and hauled himself to his feet.

J.C. rose at once, taking the man's arm as he moved toward the bench. "Sir, people don't get dizzy without a reason." He could hear the ambulance siren now. Maneuvering the large vehicle through the jammed, narrow streets would take a few minutes, however. And he wanted to keep the man talking until the EMTs arrived.

"There's a reason." The older gentleman winced as he put his weight on his right leg, and J.C. tightened his grip. "I must have bruised my knee."

"The EMTs can check that out, too."

"Maybe." The man settled onto the bench. "I have a nonrefundable plane ticket for next Tuesday, and I do need to be able to navigate through the airport. I suppose you have to fill out some kind of report?"

"Yes." J.C. pulled out his notebook and pen. "Let's start with your name."

"Walter Anderson."

J.C.'s fingers froze as he shot him a startled look.

One of the man's eyebrows rose. "Do we know each other?"

"No, sir. But I know your daughter."

Now it was Walter's turn to look surprised. "You know Heather?"

"Yes. We're neighbors." Still taken aback by the odd coincidence, J.C. tried to refocus on the task at hand. "Let me get a little more information for my report."

By the time he'd obtained a local address, a phone number and other pertinent facts, the ambulance was rolling to a stop at the curb.

"Is there anyone you'd like me to notify about this?"

Walter hesitated, then shook his head. "No. Thank you."

The EMTs joined them, and J.C. rose. After giving them a quick recap of the situation, he stepped aside.

And even though Heather's father hadn't asked him to place any calls, he pulled out his cell phone.

It had to be here.

Rummaging through the drawer in her mother's nightstand, Heather felt a momentary flutter of panic—until at last her fingers closed over the leather-bound Bible that had never been far from Barbara Anderson during the final days of her life.

After pulling it into the light from the dark drawer where it had lain for two years, she searched for the passage from Ephesians that J.C. had referenced. She hoped the book her mother had put such stock in would offer her some guidance. That was where J.C. always seemed to turn for answers, too.

Finding the verses he'd referenced, she sat in the chair in the corner of her mother's room and read through them.

"All bitterness, fury, anger, shouting and reviling must be removed from you, along with all malice. Be kind to one another, compassionate, forgiving one another as God has forgiven you in Christ."

Good advice, Heather acknowledged. But how did you get past the hurt to follow it?

As she flipped idly through the book, pondering

that question, a folded sheet of paper fluttered to the floor. It was covered with the graceful flow of her mother's handwriting, and Heather's throat tightened. Barbara Anderson had always had beautiful penmanship. But based on the shaky script, this must have been written very near the end of her life.

When she bent to retrieve it, Heather saw that it was a letter. And the salutation startled her.

It was addressed to her father.

Heart hammering, she began to read.

Dear Walter,

I'm sure this letter will surprise you. It surprised me, too. But after recently finding my way to the Lord, I've been forced to face some hard facts about myself.

The truth is, I wasn't always easy to live with during our marriage. I had too much stubbornness. Too much self-righteousness. Too much need for control.

I'm sorry I couldn't find the courage to release you from a job you hated. To set you free to follow your dream. And I'm sorry for the terrible things I said the night of your reunion.

Most of all, I'm sorry I couldn't find it in my heart to forgive you—and to work through our problems. I'm sorry, too, that once we parted, my pride kept me from changing my mind.

I also carry great guilt about your estrangement from Heather. I should have encouraged her to stay in touch with you. Instead, I accepted her loyalty to me as a validation of my actions. But that was wrong. She loved you, Walter. And she needed you. I plan to talk with her about us in the next few days. And try to set the stage for a reconciliation.

Please know that I have many regrets about what happened to us. With each passing year, it's become more clear to me what I lost when we parted. Your kindness and caring were blessings I took…

The letter ended abruptly. Unfinished.

Rereading the words her mother had penned, Heather was forced to acknowledge that everything Susan and Edith had told her was true. There had been major issues in her parents' marriage. And while her father had made a terrible mistake, her mother wasn't without blame for the problems in their relationship.

A jarring ring shattered the stillness in the house, and her hand jerked. Clutching the letter, she hurried down the hall to her bedroom and grabbed the phone off the nightstand. "The Devon Rose."

"Heather? It's J.C."

His serious tone penetrated her preoccupation, and she sucked in a sharp breath. "Is everything okay?"

"I think so. But I wanted to let you know your

dad fell downtown a few minutes ago. They took him to the E.R. to get checked out, but as far as I could tell, he was okay except for a banged-up knee."

Groping for the bed behind her, she sank down and closed her eyes. "Did he ask you to call me?"

"No. But there are a few other things you should know. He's staying at Star of the Sea."

The youth hostel in Surfside? Miles from town, where bare-bones rooms were shared with several other people?

"Also, he didn't rent a car, so he's been taking the Shuttle."

This was getting worse by the minute.

"And he's not leaving until next Tuesday. He has a nonrefundable ticket."

Her father was going to be around for five more days. With an injured knee. And in obvious need of assistance.

Heather closed her eyes. The moment of truth had been thrust upon her, ready or not. She could ignore her father, as she had for twenty long years. Or she could take the high road and start down the path to forgiveness.

Heather knew what J.C. would advise. Her mother would concur, she suspected, fingering the letter in her hand. And so would the Lord.

Making her decision, she took the leap. "Okay. I'm on my way to the E.R."

Chapter Fourteen

"Ms. Anderson?"

Heather looked up from the magazine she'd been aimlessly paging through in the E.R. The doctor she'd been introduced to at the fence painting youth project in 'Sconset stood a few feet away.

"Hello, Dr. Morgan."

A smile of recognition lifted his lips. Moving across the room, he extended his hand as he claimed the seat beside her. "It's nice to see you again. Although I'm sorry it's under these circumstances. But the good news is that your father's knee is only bruised. In a few days the soreness and stiffness will dissipate. He may need a little help in the interim, though."

"I plan to have him stay with me for the remainder of his visit. Can he do steps?"

"Yes. Slowly, and with assistance."

"Does he know I'm here?"

"Yes. Would you like to come back and see him?"

What she'd like to do was run the other direction. But she'd already made her decision. "Yes."

She followed him into the E.R., where he indicated a half-closed door before moving on. "Take your time."

Drawing a fortifying breath, Heather gave a light tap and stepped inside.

Her father stood across the room, one hand resting on the examining table as if to steady himself, looking pale and every bit his seventy years.

"I'm sorry to trouble you with this, Heather." His stance was rigid, his shoulders taut. "I didn't ask anyone to call you."

"I know. I understand you're staying at Star of the Sea."

He shifted his weight, and the paper beneath his hand on the examining table crinkled. "Yes."

Folding her arms across her chest, Heather wrapped her fingers around her upper arms and held on as her heart began to pound. "I have a spare room at The Devon Rose. It's yours if you want to use it."

In the silence that followed, Walter gave a slow blink. His Adam's apple bobbed. Moisture shone in his eyes. "I'd like that. Thank you." His words came out choked.

Her own throat tightened with emotion, and she

turned to open the door, struggling to regain control. "Okay. Let's go get your things."

Using the examining table for support, he took a step forward. Winced. Took another. Winced again. Shot her an apologetic look.

"Sorry. I bruised my knee when I fell."

"The doctor told me." Fighting down a flutter of nerves, she moved beside him and crooked her elbow in his direction. "Why don't you hold on to me?"

He hesitated, searching her face. It was impossible to miss the hope shining in his blue irises as he slipped his arm through hers.

Once upon a time, she'd leaned on him, she recalled with a wistful pang as they slowly traversed the hall to the waiting room. Looked up to him, both literally and figuratively. He no longer seemed as tall as he once had. Or as strong. Or as perfect. Those illusions were gone.

And yet…with his arm in hers, life felt complete for the first time in twenty years.

Brian was waiting for them at The Devon Rose. She'd called him from the E.R. after she knew he'd be back from a youth group sailing outing, and as she braked to a stop, she heard the screen door bang. A few seconds later, he loped around the car, coming to a stop beside the passenger door. Pulling it open, he helped his grandfather out, then engulfed him in a bear hug.

As the two embraced, Heather backed off a few steps—and ran into a solid chest. Firm hands closed over her upper arms, steadying her, and she twisted around.

J.C.

"I thought you might need a little moral support."

His husky voice, and the tenderness in his eyes, played havoc with her breathing.

"Thank you."

He gave her arms a squeeze and moved toward the car. "Hello, Mr. Anderson."

Her father gave him a surprised look. "Aren't you the officer who helped me today?"

J.C. grinned. "Yes."

"You look different." He eyed J.C.'s jeans and black T-shirt.

So did Heather.

"Civvies always throw people off. Brian, why don't you and I take your grandfather's bags upstairs?"

As they collected the luggage, her father looked from J.C. to her, and Heather felt warmth steal across her cheeks. Walter Anderson might have aged, but she had a feeling his keen perceptive abilities hadn't diminished one iota.

With the two younger males handling the luggage, Heather knew her father would need her arm again. Closing the distance between them, she offered it.

"Nice young man," he remarked as they navigated the brick walkway.

"He's been very good with Brian."

"I can see that. Your sister tells me he's turned a corner since he's been here. I'm glad you girls have always…"

"Hey, Aunt Heather, are you fixing dinner?" Brian banged through the door, back onto the porch, J.C. close behind. "I'm starved."

It was dinnertime, she realized. But no way was she up to cooking tonight. "I could order pizza."

"Cool!" Brian replied. "You wanna stay, J.C.?"

When J.C. sent her a questioning glance, she seconded Brian's invitation. "Please."

"Thanks. That sounds good." He came down the steps and took up a position on the other side of her father. "A couple of steps, here, sir."

"Call me Walter."

"And I'm J.C. Let's take it slow and easy."

With support on both sides, he ascended with no problem.

And as her father stepped into The Devon Rose, his arm linked with hers, Heather knew they were also stepping into a new chapter in their lives.

An hour later, Brian snagged the last piece of pizza. "Anybody want this?"

Heather shook her head. "I'm done."

"Me, too." J.C. wiped his hands on a napkin.

"Grandpa?"

"It's all yours, Brian."

Tipping his head back, J.C. emptied his soft-drink can and stood. "I think I'm ready to call it a day. Can I give you a hand upstairs, Walter?"

"Thank you. I'd appreciate it."

"I'll go with you and show you the room, Grandpa." Brian shoved the last bite of pizza in his mouth and rose.

Walter stood, too. "Good night, Heather."

"Good night."

Brian kept up a steady chatter as the three of them slowly ascended the staircase to the second floor, but once Walter was ensconced in his room, J.C. headed back to the kitchen. He'd been watching Heather all night. And while she'd been holding up well, the tense line of her mouth and the faint tremor in her hands were telling. He didn't know that he could do much to relieve her stress—but he could at least offer to provide whatever practical assistance she might need…or an ear for venting.

He found her in the kitchen, clearing up the remains of the impromptu dinner.

She gave him an apologetic look as he entered. "You've really gotten more than you bargained for with this family, haven't you?"

"There have been some redeeming factors." Without giving her a chance to dwell on that, he gestured toward the door. "Walk with me to the gate?"

"Sure." She wiped her hands on a towel and pushed through the door.

As she moved down the brick path at the edge of

her garden, J.C. fell into step beside her. The manicured, formal display of shrubs and flowers was immaculate, as always, he noted. Pristine, well-ordered, symmetrical, balanced. A direct contrast to her chaotic life of late.

As if reading his mind, Heather bent to pluck a stray weed from the edge of the boxwood border. "Too bad it's not this easy to get rid of the bad stuff in life."

"You've had more than your share of that lately." He touched her arm, and she stopped. "I want you to know I admire what you've done with Brian and your dad. That took a lot of courage."

She shoved her hands into the pockets of her jeans and shook her head. "I feel more scared than brave."

When he reached over and brushed his fingers against her cheek, her sharp indrawn breath echoed in the quiet of the garden. "Don't be scared. You're doing fine. But if you ever need any backup, I'm available."

She looked up at him, searching his eyes in the deepening dusk. "Why are you getting so involved in my mess? I thought you wanted an uncomplicated stay on Nantucket to work through your own issues?"

"I did. But a beautiful woman with incredible hazel eyes and a caring, compassionate heart sucked me in."

At his admission, awareness between them heightened. He watched as longing softened Heather's features, even as she tried to fight it.

"I thought we were going to avoid…this."

"So did I."

"This isn't a good idea, J.C. You're leaving in six weeks. You have enough on your plate. And I already told you I don't trust my judgment when it comes to men."

"I know."

"We should pull back."

"I know."

And he did. But as he stood beside Heather in the quiet Nantucket garden she loved, he could no longer ignore the attraction that had quivered between them from the day he'd first set foot in The Devon Rose. An attraction that had blossomed into a deep emotional connection.

In the weeks since that fateful meeting, he'd discovered she was smart and strong and kind. That her compassion ran deep. That she wasn't too proud to admit she'd been wrong. She was the kind of woman who brought out the best in a man. A woman who had earned his respect, admiration and deepest affection.

And perhaps his love.

J.C. wasn't yet ready to take that final step. But neither could he ignore the yearning in Heather's eyes—and in his heart.

Closing the distance between them, he framed her face with his hands. And there, in the stillness of a Nantucket night, he claimed her lips.

J.C. didn't want the kiss to end. And it was clear

Heather didn't, either. But when it began to deepen, he was the one who drew back. While he could.

For several seconds, as he held her close, neither of them spoke. Then, exhaling a soft sigh, she eased back.

He let her go.

Reluctantly.

"I'm not sure that was smart." She tucked her hair behind her ear and inspected his T-shirt.

"Are you sorry?"

When she lifted her head, her eyes were steady. And sure. "No. But it complicates things even more. And I have other issues to deal with at the moment."

He tried for a smile. "Then let's table this for a few days, until things settle down."

She gave a slow nod. "Okay."

Leaning close, he brushed his lips across her forehead. "One for the road," he murmured.

With a final caress of her cheek, he let himself out through the gate.

As he walked the short distance back to his cottage, J.C. braced for the doubts he was certain would assail him. For the twinge of regret he expected to feel.

Instead, all he felt was happy.

Meaning that in the next six weeks, he had some serious thinking to do about the future of a certain Chicago cop.

Chapter Fifteen

Give it up.

With a resigned sigh, Heather threw back the covers and stood. With her father under her roof and J.C. making inroads on her heart, the few fitful hours of sleep she'd clocked since that kiss in the garden were all she was going to manage. She might as well get an early start on her baking.

An hour later, as she slid the first batch of scones into the oven, the sound of running water upstairs alerted her that her father was up. Wiping her floury hands on a dish towel, she headed for the foyer. The last thing she needed was for him to get dizzy and take a tumble down the stairs.

He was exiting the bathroom as she reached the landing, already dressed in a pair of beige paints and a dark green shirt. He gave her a tentative smile. "Good morning, Heather."

She acknowledged his greeting with a dip of her head. "Would you like some breakfast?"

"All I need is toast and coffee." He inspected her voluminous apron, already smudged with flour and chocolate. "I was thinking last night—maybe we could set aside some time to talk on Monday, when the tearoom is closed. I know how busy you must be running this place single-handedly."

She liked that plan. It would give her a chance to get more comfortable in his presence before they dived into the heavy stuff. "Okay. Are you ready to go down?"

"Yes." He took her arm with one hand, steadying himself on the banister with the other and favoring his sore knee as they descended.

Once in the kitchen, he insisted on preparing his own simple breakfast, shooing her back to work. Although she was conscious of the glances he sent her way as he ate at the small oak table, he didn't attempt to start a conversation.

Things got livelier once Brian joined them. The two men in her house enjoyed a spirited game of checkers, and after Brian went off to surf, her father took a book to the garden. J.C. dropped over, too, and at Heather's invitation, he joined them for dinner again.

To Heather's relief, the weekend passed with far less tension than she'd expected. Her father played the role of houseguest with consummate ease, pitching in with the dishes, straightening up after himself, engaging in light, pleasant conversation when J.C., Edith and Chester dropped by. And his rapport with Brian, underscored by deep affection on both sides, warmed—and softened—Heather's heart.

In the end, she was forced to admit her sister and Brian had been right.

Her father was a good man.

On Sunday night, as they cleaned up after dinner, J.C. drew her aside. "I'm off tomorrow. A makeup day for the holiday. Would you like me to keep Brian occupied?"

She'd told him that Monday was D-day with her father, and she gave him a grateful look. "Are you sure you don't mind?"

"No. One of the guys at work is into deep-sea fishing. I thought Brian might enjoy that. I could take him out for pizza afterward."

Hot tears pricked her eyes. "You're amazing."

He gave her that half-hitch grin she loved. "Hold that thought."

She did. And it kept her awake half the night.

But as she tossed in the dark early-morning hours, it was the coming encounter with her father that kept her as restless as the tide.

He was waiting when she came out of her bedroom the next morning, sitting in a chair near the top of the stairs, a small Bible in his hand. And he didn't appear any more rested than she felt.

He closed the Bible. "Good morning."

"Good morning. If it's okay with you, I thought we could grab some doughnuts and coffee at

Downyflake and head to one of my favorite spots on the island. It would be a good place to talk."

"That sounds fine to me."

Half an hour later, Heather pulled the car to a stop at her favorite access point to Ladies Beach. Slinging a tote bag over her shoulder, she juggled the cardboard tray of coffee and a bag of doughnuts as she offered her father an arm. After selecting a spot in the shelter of a dune, she spread out two large beach towels, helped him sit and passed out the food and drink.

As she'd hoped, the two of them were the sole occupants of this stretch of windswept beach. Sipping the steaming liquid, she let the familiar peace seep into her soul. The cerulean water sparkled in the morning sun, as if sprinkled with diamonds, and she drew in a cleansing breath of the tangy salt air. She watched a sandpiper play tag with the surf. Listened to the caw of a gull high overhead and the muted thunder of the breaking waves. Felt the breeze caress her cheek.

Turning to her father, she found him in a similar contemplative mood, his gaze fixed on the distant horizon.

As if sensing her perusal, he looked her way. "This is a perfect spot."

A melancholy smile touched her lips. "I don't know if I'll ever use that word again. The pursuit of perfection can be disheartening. And expecting perfection only leads to disappointment."

He examined the lid of his cup. "You certainly didn't have an example of perfection in me."

She shook her head. "I wasn't talking about you. I was thinking of myself. And, to be honest, Mom." She ran her fingers through the sand. Swallowed. "I've learned some things recently that have given me a new perspective on what happened twenty years ago. From Susan. And Edith. And from Mom." Shaking the grains from her fingers, she withdrew her mother's half-written letter from the tote bag and held it out to him. "I found this a few days ago in Mom's Bible. I think you should read it."

Walter regarded the folded sheet of paper. "I don't know what that is, Heather. And I don't know what you learned. But nothing changes the fact that I made a huge mistake that destroyed our family."

"You did make a mistake, Dad. But I'm beginning to think it didn't have to destroy our family." She moved the letter closer and gentled her tone. "Please. Read this first."

Aiming a speculative look at her, he set his coffee cup back in the cardboard tray and withdrew his glasses from the case in his shirt pocket. A quiver ran through his hand as he took the sheet of paper, unfolded it and began to read.

Heather watched him as he gave the letter his full attention, noting the faint tremor in his lips, the subtle twitch of the muscles in his jaw, the moisture gathering at the corners of his eyes. She knew what he was thinking. It was the same thought she'd had when she'd read the letter, after the initial shock had passed.

If only...

But the past couldn't be changed. All they could do was look to the future. And she at last felt ready to do that.

After he finished reading, he refolded the sheet of paper and brushed a hand across his eyes.

"I wish I'd known all that years ago," Heather said softly. "And that I'd let Susan talk to me about you and Mom and the problems you had. I never knew about the job issue."

"You discovered everything when you were meant to." He reached over and grasped her hand with the strong, solid grip she remembered. The one that had guided her back onto the dance floor so many years ago and restored her self-esteem and confidence. "Besides, it doesn't change the speech I've been waiting to give for twenty years. It just saves me from having to provide as much background."

Releasing her hand, he laced his fingers tightly around one knee and looked into her eyes, letting her see all his pain and regret and contrition.

"As you've discovered, your mom and I had different views on life. I wanted to strike out on a new career. She thought it was too risky. And she was right. I had a home and family to think about. Opening a bookstore was a selfish dream. But I couldn't see that back then. On the day of my reunion, we had a huge argument about it."

Walter took a deep breath, his features flexing with anguish. "I went to the reunion alone. Drank way too much alcohol. Found a sympathetic ear in a divorced classmate. You know the rest." He wiped a hand wearily down his face and picked up the letter again. "I hoped your mother might forgive me, but I understood when she couldn't. No matter what this letter says, I'm the one who destroyed our family. And I want you to know not a day has passed that I haven't regretted my terrible mistake. I'm so sorry, Heather. So sorry."

At his choked expression of remorse, Heather's heart contracted. As she had done for two decades, her father had put the blame for the destruction of his marriage and his family squarely—and solely—on his shoulders.

But she didn't see it that way anymore.

Some of the blame rested on her mother.

And a lot rested on her.

If she'd been willing years ago to listen to his side of the story, to find a way to forgive him, she might not have been able to put her family back together again. But the father she'd loved—and who'd never stopped loving her—could have been part of her life.

The thought of all those wasted years twisted her stomach into a knot.

Reaching over, she squeezed his fingers. "I know, Dad. And I also know the fault wasn't only yours. I'm sorry I couldn't see that sooner." Tears shook her voice, and she swallowed.

Relief and gratitude smoothed some of the tension from his features. But regret remained. "And I wish I'd pushed the issue long ago. But I was afraid you'd reject me again, and I couldn't face that. I guess that's one positive that came out of the brain tumor. It gave me the courage to come here."

Her hand tightened on his. "Susan says the prognosis is good."

"It is. But surgery always carries some risk. And I didn't want to leave this world without making one more attempt to mend our relationship." He gave her a tremulous smile. "I'm glad I did."

She managed the whisper of a smile, too. "So am I."

"You know, we have a lot of catching up to do."

"I have all day."

"I do, too."

And so they sat there for hours, Heather filling him in on her life on Nantucket, while Walter told her of his gratifying but lonely years as a bookseller. They talked until the sun began to dip, until at last hunger compelled them to pack up and head back to the car. After picking up sandwiches at Bartlett's Farm, they toured the rest of the island, finishing their day by watching the famous sunset at Madaket Beach.

When at last they returned to The Devon Rose and ascended the steps, he turned to her. "It was a good day, Heather. Thank you."

"It was a good day for me, too."

"Can I give you a hug?"

"I'll be disappointed if you don't."

He reached for her then, pulling her into arms that no longer had the strength of youth or the power of an invincible superhero. Instead, they were the welcoming, sheltering arms of a father who might not be perfect, but whose love had endured even in the face of rejection.

And that was enough.

"Hey, J.C. Got a minute?"

Glancing up as he exited the large room near the front of the station where the summer special officers hung out, J.C. saw Burke standing in the door of his office, a disposable cup in his hand. In his Chicago days, Burke had never been far from a swig of java. Some things never changed.

"Sure."

To J.C.'s surprise, Dan Holden, head of the detective division, was in the office, too. In his short stay on the island, Dan had called on him a few times for assistance with a case.

"Have a seat." Burke gestured to a vacant chair as he rounded his desk and took his own seat. "Joe Martin informed us a few days ago that he plans to take early retirement in October. We'll be looking for a good detective to replace him. Any interest?"

Burke was offering him a job.

Stunned, J.C. tried to process this unexpected

turn of events. He'd always looked upon this job as temporary. Yet the appeal of his old life in Chicago had faded over the summer. In truth, he was tired of dealing with the gritty side of life. Tired of the politics in a big-city police department. Tired of never knowing when he left for work in the morning if he'd end up on a slab in the morgue.

Nantucket was a whole different world. Sure, there were some shady characters here. Yes, there was small-town politics. But he didn't feel as if he had to watch his back every minute. And he liked dealing with people who appreciated his assistance, who thanked him for his efforts and who often shook his hand after he resolved an incident.

It had other attractions, too. Including a lovely tearoom owner.

"At least he didn't say no right away."

At Dan's amused comment, J.C. rejoined the conversation. "I might be interested. It depends on a few…personal things."

"That's good enough for today. I just wanted to plant the seed." Burke's phone began to ring, and the two other men rose as he reached for it.

J.C. followed Dan into the hall. "I appreciate you and Burke thinking of me for the vacancy."

The other man waved his gratitude aside and continued toward the steps to the second floor. "It's good to find competent people."

Flattered by the compliment, J.C. exited and headed south to his assigned sector for foot patrol, mulling over the offer. When he'd come to Nantucket, he'd been praying for guidance, answers and release from guilt. The guilt was largely gone, and he'd gotten some answers. Perhaps the job offer was the guidance he'd been seeking. Maybe it was a sign that it was time to leave his old life behind.

And start a new one on this windswept island, with the woman who had stolen his heart.

"It's a teacup, Aunt Heather. J.C. and I picked it out yesterday at an antique store on our way back from fishing. I'm going to send you another one at Christmas. Maybe by the time I go to college, I'll be able to replace all the ones I broke."

Heather looked down at the wrapped package Brian had thrust into her hands as they waited in the airport for the flight that would take him and his grandfather back to St. Louis. What a change from the sullen teen who'd arrived a little over three weeks ago, she reflected.

"Thank you, Brian."

The loudspeaker boomed, announcing their flight, and Heather motioned toward her father, who was seated nearby. "Take care of your grandfather on the way home, okay?"

"Sure. And I'm really glad you decided to talk to him. Now we can all be a family again."

"I'm glad, too."

Brian shot the older man an anxious look. "I think he's gonna be okay, don't you?"

She hoped so. "It sounds very promising."

"Yeah. That's what I thought."

As Walter rose and picked up his carry-on, Heather moved beside him. "Be safe, Dad." She reached out, and he gave her a tight hug.

"I will. And I'm going to take you up on your invitation to come back at Christmas."

She smiled. "That would be great." Turning to Brian, she hugged him, too. "Stay out of trouble, okay?"

"Yeah. I'm done with that stuff. Come on, Grandpa." He took the older man's arm, and they moved off.

Heather watched until they'd disappeared from sight. Then she pulled out her cell phone to call J.C. Though he'd offered to try to find a replacement at work so he could accompany her to the airport, she'd assured him she'd be fine. And she was.

But she'd be better after she heard his voice.

Because she was falling in love with him.

As she tapped in his number, a thrill ran through her. Yet she was also scared. Things were moving too fast. She'd had a whirlwind courtship with Mark, and look how that had ended.

But that relationship had been different, she thought as she waited for J.C. to answer. With Mark, she'd always been in control of her emotions. Able to weigh the pros and cons of caring for him and to dole out her affection in safe increments as she tested the waters. Tested him.

Maybe that was one of the reasons it hadn't worked, she conceded. Perhaps Mark had never felt needed. Or important in her life.

And the truth was, he hadn't been.

That role belonged to a special Chicago cop.

She'd told J.C. a few days ago that she didn't trust her judgment when it came to men. But she did now—with him. With his kindness and honor and humor, he'd opened the door to a new world for her. A world where trust and commitment and love beckoned. And she was ready now to take the first steps through that door…with him by her side.

Thanks to him, she was also laying the groundwork for a faith that, while still in its infancy, seemed to be pointing her toward a better way of living. Toward a new, higher relationship that would help sustain her all the days of her life.

"Heather?"

As his voice came over the line, she found herself smiling. "Hi."

"Did they get off okay?"

"Yes."

"How are you doing?"

"Better than I thought."

"Good. Listen, you deserve a night out after everything that's been going on. How about we use that gift card from the trivia event? I'd take you tonight, but I agreed to work part of the night shift for one of the guys whose wife just had a baby. Is tomorrow okay?"

"Are you asking me out on a date, Officer Clay?" Heather teased.

"Yeah. It's about time, don't you think?"

She chuckled. "Yeah. I'd say it's about time."

Chapter Sixteen

It was too early in the morning for the phone to be ringing.

With a groan, J.C. lifted his wrist and squinted at the numbers on his watch.

Ten-fifteen.

Okay, so it wasn't too early for phone calls. For most people. But after working a full shift yesterday and half a shift last night, he'd been in bed for less than sixty minutes.

The temptation to let the call roll to his voice mail was strong. But he wasn't wired that way.

Shifting onto his side, he groped on the nightstand for his phone and peered at the caller ID. The area code told him the call was from Illinois, but the number was unfamiliar.

Stifling a yawn, he put the phone to his ear. "Hello."

"Detective Clay?"

Few people outside work addressed him by his Chicago PD title. Caution colored his response. "Yes."

"This is Eric Coplin, the warden at Pontiac Correctional Center. You're listed as the primary contact for your brother, Nathan. I wanted to inform you that we have your brother on suicide watch after he attempted to take his life last night."

Shock reverberated through J.C. "Is he all right?"

"Physically, yes."

"What happened?"

"He tried to strangle himself with the drawstring from his pants."

A wave of nausea swept over J.C., and he bunched the sheet in his hand as he took a long, slow breath. "Does anyone have any idea what prompted this?"

"No. And your brother isn't communicating. I've spoken with our mental health people, and they think having family close by could be helpful."

Swinging his legs out of bed, J.C. retrieved his duffel bag from the closet. "Did he ask you to call me?"

"No. He hasn't spoken more than a few words since this happened."

"Okay. I'm working on Nantucket for the summer. I'll book the first possible flight out, but I doubt I can get there in less than ten or twelve hours."

"Is there anyone closer who could come sooner?"

He thought of Marci. But she and Nathan hadn't spoken in years. There was no way she'd make the two-hour drive to Pontiac.

"No. I'll be there as soon as I can. Look…keep him safe, okay?" His voice rasped on the last word.

"We video monitor the suicide-watch cells twenty-four hours a day. Nothing will happen to him there. Shall we tell him you're coming?"

"No. I'd rather just show up."

"All right. We'll see you soon."

When the call ended, J.C. went into action. Within minutes he'd booked a flight that would leave Nantucket for Boston in an hour and a half. Factoring in a two-hour layover there, he'd arrive in Chicago about five. Thanks to rush-hour traffic in the Windy City on a Friday afternoon, the usual two-hour drive to Pontiac would take longer. Plus, he needed to pick up a rental car. Best-case scenario, he estimated arrival at Pontiac around eight.

Next, he called Burke. He knew cutting out on short notice was going to put everyone in a bind, but he had no option. Fortunately, the chief was familiar with his family situation. Or as much of it as J.C. had ever shared with anyone. Burke simply told him to do what he had to do and come back when he could.

Ending that call, J.C. tossed his duffel bag onto the bed and punched in Marci's number. She might not want any part of this mess, but he figured she should know what had happened.

She answered as he began opening the drawers in his dresser and tossing clothes into the bag.

"Marci, I just had a call from Pontiac." His tone was clipped, his mind racing ahead to the logistics of the trip. "I know there's no love lost between you and Nathan, but I thought you should know. He tried to kill himself last night."

He heard her draw a harsh breath. "Oh, God!" The agonized whisper was torn from the depths of her soul.

Surprised at her reaction, J.C. stopped packing. She hadn't expressed one iota of sympathy for Nathan in years. Nor had she ever asked about him. The anguish in her inflection didn't fit.

"Marci? Are you okay?"

A choked sob came over the line. The words that followed were barely audible. "I was afraid this would happen."

"What are you talking about?"

"After you told me the news about the drug bust, I—I wrote him. It wasn't a nice letter. I beat him up pretty bad for almost getting you killed. And I told him about the two cops who died."

"What!" The word exploded from J.C.'s lips, and the churning in his gut intensified.

"I—I'm sorry, J.C." Marci's whispered apology caught on a sob. "I was just so mad about the way he's treated you, after all you've done to try to help him. But as soon as I m-mailed the letter, I had a feeling it was a mistake."

Raking his fingers through his hair, J.C. tried to regroup. What was done was done, he reminded himself. It was clear Marci regretted her rash action, and berating her wasn't going to change the situation. It would only strain a relationship he'd worked hard to solidify.

And one good thing had come out of this, he suddenly realized. If Marci's letter had driven Nathan to take this drastic measure, it must mean his brother hadn't purposely set him up. Otherwise, he wouldn't have felt any guilt or remorse.

"Okay." J.C. swallowed. "We can't rewind. We have what we have. I'm heading back in about an hour and a half. I'll let you know how everything goes."

"Are you... How are you getting to Pontiac?"

"I'll get a rental at O'Hare." He resumed packing.

"Why don't I pick you up? We could drive down together."

J.C.'s hand froze as he tucked a pair of socks into the duffel. "You want to go with me?"

"No." Her breath hitched. "But I have to. This is my fault, J.C. I can't just walk away from that responsibility."

He didn't try to reassure her or absolve her of blame. They both knew her letter had been the catalyst for this crisis.

"Okay." He gave her his flight information, tossed his shaving kit into the duffel and zipped the bag closed. "I'll see you in a few hours."

Checking his watch as he ended the call, J.C. picked up his Bible. He needed five minutes with the twenty-third Psalm. Then he'd order a cab, run over and talk to Heather, and try to prepare for the difficult hours ahead.

As a knock sounded on her back door, Heather slid the tray of lemon tarts she was holding on to a cooling rack and turned. To her surprise, J.C. stood in the shadows of the porch. She'd expected him to sleep late today.

"Come on in." Smiling, she walked toward him as he pulled open the door and stepped through.

When the bright kitchen light illuminated his face, however, her step faltered. He looked as if someone had died.

Picking up her pace again, she covered the distance between them in a few long strides and reached for his hands. "What's wrong?"

His grip was fierce. "Nathan tried to commit suicide last night."

Shock wiped the expression from her face. "Oh, J.C.! Is he going to be okay?"

"Yeah. But I'm heading back there to be with him."

"Of course. What happened?"

"Marci sent him a letter. I told her about Nathan's role in the drug bust ambush, and she decided to let him have it. Listen…I'm sorry about canceling our date tonight."

"I'll give you a rain check." Heather loosened her hand and reached up to touch his cheek. "Do you… Would you like some company on your trip?"

She saw surprise flare in his eyes—followed by a flame of love shining strong and bright in their depths. Just as she knew it was shining in hers.

"You'll never know how much that offer means to me." His voice hoarsened, and he cleared his throat. "But your life has been thrown into chaos enough lately. And you have a business to run."

"This is more important."

He touched her face, stroked her hair, let his hand drift down to cup her neck. "I'll be okay. As long as I know you're waiting when I return."

She took a step closer and put her arms around his neck. "Count on it."

He rested his hands on her waist and searched her eyes. "There's a lot I want to talk about when I get back."

"I'll be here. What time is your flight?"

"In just over an hour. I need to go."

"Let me drive you."

"A cab's already on the way." She started to protest, but he lifted a hand. "I'd rather say goodbye here."

With that, he bent his head and gave her a lingering kiss.

When at last he drew back, he stroked her cheek with a fingertip. "Say a few prayers, okay?"

"I'll say more than a few."

He gave her one more hug, then stepped out the door.

And as he disappeared around the house, she

knew he would need every prayer he could get to make it through the traumatic hours to come.

By the time Marci and J.C. pulled up ten hours later in front of the dreary stone structure Nathan called home, his eyes felt gritty with fatigue. And the harsh lights in the sterile conference room they were shown to didn't help.

Two people were waiting for them. He knew Steve Taylor, the chaplain. They'd often spoken during his visits. The thirtysomething woman with gold-rimmed glasses and short brown hair, who introduced herself as Jo Sherman, chief of psychology services at the facility, was a stranger.

After providing them with cups of strong coffee, the psychologist took the lead. "Before you see Nathan, we wanted you to know we think we've found the trigger for his actions."

She opened a folder and withdrew a letter. J.C. recognized Marci's handwriting at once. Beside him, coffee sloshed on the table as his sister's grip tightened on her disposable cup.

"We came to the same conclusion." J.C. used his napkin to mop up the spilled liquid.

The psychologist folded her hands on the table and leaned forward intently. "As bad as everything seems right now, there is a plus side. Nathan's despondency over this letter and his subsequent suicide attempt indicate a well-formed conscience. He cares about the repercussions of his actions. That has positive implications for rehabilitation."

"Only if we can get him to care about living again." J.C. compressed his lips into a grim line.

"I think you're the one who can do that," the psychologist said.

J.C. shook his head, a pang of regret echoing in his heart. "He has no use for me."

The psychologist gave him a long look, then pulled a small plastic bin toward her. "We found this when his cell was inspected after the suicide attempt." Opening the lid, she withdrew several notebooks and set them on the table. Underneath, lined up in neat rows, were letters.

His letters, J.C. realized.

Dozens and dozens of them.

He stared at them, stunned, as she silently pushed the bin toward him.

With fingers that weren't quite steady, he riffled through them. They'd been filed in chronological order, the older ones yellowed a bit, he noted. Pulling out the first one, he checked the date. Sucked in a sharp breath. Closed his eyes.

Nathan had kept every single letter he'd written.

And based on their dog-eared appearance, each had been read numerous times.

"We also found these in the bin." The psychologist gestured toward the notebooks. Selecting the one on top, she opened it to the first page and handed it to J.C.

Another shock rippled through him. The pencil portrait took several years off his age, but it had been rendered in exquisite, loving detail by a masterful hand.

Paging through the rest of the notebook, he found more portraits—including one of Marci, which elicited a soft gasp from his sister—plus still-life scenes and a few landscapes. All were beautifully executed.

"There are five more notebooks like that," the psychologist told him.

J.C. shook his head, overwhelmed. "I had no idea."

"Nathan has a remarkable talent—and a lot to offer," the chaplain said. "Our challenge is to convince him of that."

Wiping a hand down his face, J.C. sighed. "How do we do that?" He felt no closer to answering that troubling question now than he had when Nathan had first been incarcerated.

"I wish I had the magic words that would reach into his heart and convince him he's loved and valued not only by his family but by the Lord," the chaplain said. "I've tried, but he's never been receptive to that message. Perhaps he will be now. Why don't we ask God to give you the words that will help him turn his life around?"

J.C. knew Marci would be uncomfortable with prayer, but he needed the strength it would offer. "That's a good idea."

With a nod, the chaplain bowed his head. "Lord, please be with J.C. and Marci as they talk to Nathan. Help him hear their message with his heart as well as his ears. Let him believe in their enduring love. And let him feel Your healing grace so that in time he may be open to Your words. Amen."

When the prayer ended, J.C. looked at Marci. "Do you want to go in together?"

She shook her head. "You go first. Two of us at once might overwhelm him."

"I arranged for you to see Nathan in one of the private interview rooms," the psychologist told him. "There will be guards present, but the atmosphere will be more conducive to interpersonal interaction."

That was a deviation from the usual rigid security protocol, J.C. knew. Perhaps his law enforcement credentials had bought them a few concessions. Whatever the reason, he was grateful. "Thank you."

Five minutes later, when he entered the small room, Nathan was already there, two guards standing nearby. In place of the usual orange prison garb, he wore a blue, sleeveless isolation jumpsuit. The one-piece kind with Velcro fasteners, often used for prisoners on suicide watch. J.C.'s stomach clenched.

As he moved toward the table, his first thought was that the past five years hadn't been kind to his kid brother. Though he was only thirty-two, fine lines radiated from the corners of his eyes. A smattering of gray peppered his brown hair, and above his drooping shoulders, his cheeks were gaunt.

Rather than looking up when J.C. entered, he continued to stare dully at his shackled hands, folded on the table in front of him.

Swallowing past the lump in his throat, J.C. spoke. "Hello, Nathan."

His brother's head snapped up.

For one brief second, surprise added a touch of life to his flat eyes. Then the emptiness returned. Without a word, he dropped his gaze to his hands again.

A wave of panic crashed over J.C. While the anger in his brother's eyes had often frightened him, this beaten look scared him more.

Taking a seat across the table from Nathan, he sent one final, silent prayer heavenward. *Please, Lord, give me the words!*

"I saw the letters, Nathan. And the notebooks."

His brother didn't look up.

"I never knew you could draw."

No response.

Following his instincts—and praying they wouldn't fail him—J.C. changed tacks. "But I did think you were too smart to pull a dumb stunt like suicide." He let that sink in, noting the slight stiffening in Nathan's shoulders. "Do you have any idea how long it took to get here from Nantucket? Ten hours. And let me tell you, flying these days is no picnic. To make matters worse, I've had less than six hours of sleep in the past thirty-six hours. I'm tired, hungry and stressed. Trust me. I didn't come all this way to be ignored."

Nathan still didn't look up. Didn't move a muscle. But J.C. saw his Adam's apple bob. And when his brother spoke, the tremor in his muted words suggested he was barely holding on to his control.

"I didn't ask you to come."

J.C. suspected the psychologist would disapprove of his approach. Would tell him it was a bad idea to upset Nathan. But to J.C.'s way of thinking, *some* emotion was better than no emotion. It meant a person was still capable of feeling. And once feelings were awakened, you had a chance of turning them from negative to positive. His next task.

Leaning close, he laid his hand over his brother's. The guards edged in. He ignored them.

When Nathan tried to pull away, J.C. tightened his grip. And kept tightening it until Nathan looked up at him. Locking on to his brother's eyes, J.C. didn't let go. "Here's the bottom line, Nathan. I don't care how much effort it took to get here. Because you're worth it."

Disgust and self-recrimination twisted the younger man's features. He lowered his head and tried to pull away, but J.C. held fast. "No, I'm not. You should have given up on me years ago."

"I never give up on people I love."

Sudden moisture dampened the edges of Nathan's distraught eyes, and his chest began to heave. "Why don't you just let this go? I'm no good. I never have been. Everything I touch turns to trouble. My life is one big failure. I couldn't even kill myself right." His voice broke.

"I think God's hand was in that," J.C. said quietly. "He must have something better in store for you before He calls you home."

Cynicism twisted Nathan's lips. "Right. An ex-con has so much to look forward to."

"You have an extraordinary talent. When you get out of here in two years, you can choose to turn your life around. And you don't have to do it alone. You have me and Marci. As well as the Lord, if you'll give Him a chance."

There was bitterness in his brother's brief, mirthless laugh. "I have about as much chance of connecting with the Lord as I do with Marci."

"Then the odds aren't too bad."

Nathan narrowed his eyes. "What do you mean?"

"She's here."

Shock echoed on Nathan's face. "Marci came?"

"Yes. She wants to talk to you after I'm finished."

Nathan focused on J.C.'s hand, still resting atop his. The seconds ticked by. His face contorted. And then he said the words J.C. had prayed he'd hear. "Look…I'm sorry about the bust." The apology came out in a hoarse whisper. "I didn't know the guy who asked me about you had an agenda."

"I figured that was the case."

"Two people died because of me."

"It wasn't deliberate."

"That doesn't bring them back." His voice splintered.

"No. But ending your life, or wasting it, isn't going to restore theirs. It's just another life lost."

Silence hung in the room for a few moments.

"You know, all these years…I thought it would be better for you and Marci if I distanced myself." Nathan's hand spasmed, and J.C. gave it a reassuring squeeze as his brother blinked away tears. "All I ever brought the two of you was trouble. I figured you'd be better off without me. So I did everything I could to push you away. But you never gave up." He lifted his chin and studied J.C., his expression anguished and confused. "How could you keep loving me?"

"Love doesn't come with conditions, Nathan. Jesus taught us that. We didn't deserve His love, either, when He died for us on the cross. And we don't deserve it now. But He gives it, anyway, no matter how many mistakes we make. I try to follow His example."

Leaning closer, J.C. put his other hand on Nathan's shoulder. "Besides, you're my brother. I bandaged your scraped knees and cut your hair and loaned you my comic books, even if you did have a tendency to get bubble gum stuck on them. We have a lot of history. And I'd like to think we have a future, too."

The sheen was back in Nathan's eyes. "You know, I wouldn't have survived in this place without your letters." He choked out the words.

J.C. felt the pressure of tears behind his own eyes. "You better get a new box, then, because they're going to keep coming. More often, now that I know you read them."

"Promise?"

At Nathan's plaintive question, J.C. was suddenly transported back to his kid brother's kindergarten days. For the first few weeks, when J.C. had left him in the school yard and told him he'd pick him up at the end of the day, six-year-old Nathan had clung to him and issued that identical query in the same anxious tone.

"Promise." J.C. squeezed Nathan's hand. "Marci's waiting. May I send her in?"

"Yeah. We have a few fences of our own to mend."

"Would you consider talking to Reverend Taylor, too? He's a good man. With a good message to share."

Nathan gave a slow nod. "I will if it means that much to you."

"It does." J.C. rose. "I'll be back tomorrow."

A whisper of a smile tugged at Nathan's lips. "I'll be here."

That touch of humor did more to dispel the lingering knot of tension in J.C.'s stomach than anything else.

"Hang in there. We'll get through this. Together."

And as he left to get Marci, J.C. prayed Nathan would hold that last, hope-filled word close to his heart as a reminder that he would never be alone—no matter what challenges the future might hold.

Four days later, J.C. scanned the terminal, duffel bag in hand, for the woman he'd missed more than he'd thought possible. When he spotted her, dressed in a teal-green silk dress, her eyes warm with welcome, his pulse accelerated.

Erasing the distance between them, he rested his free hand on her shoulder and bent to brush his lips over hers.

"Hi." He stayed close, enjoying the play of light in her hazel irises and the sweet curve of her mouth.

"Hi."

"Thanks for picking me up. Are we still on for dinner?"

"Unless you plan to cancel again."

"Not a chance." Taking her hand, he guided her out of the terminal.

She fell into step beside him. "How's everything in Chicago?"

"Better than I expected. I'll fill you in on the drive."

By the time they parked in front of the restaurant, high on a bluff overlooking the Atlantic, he'd brought her up to speed on his family situation. That meant he had the whole dinner to focus on them. Just as he'd planned.

As the waiter showed them to their ocean-view table on the porch, soft piano music drifted through the evening air. Cascades of blue hydrangeas spilled from bushes rimming the front lawn, and appetizing aromas wafted their way from the kitchen.

"This is nice." Heather smoothed the white linen cloth with her fingers, touched the velvet-soft petals of the rose on the table, looked out over the sea. "What a great view."

"I agree."

She turned back to him, and her endearing blush when she discovered he was looking at her brought a smile to his lips.

Reaching for her hand, he entwined their fingers. "I missed you."

"I missed you, too."

"I had an interesting discussion with Burke at the station before I left." He watched her eyes. "One of the detectives is retiring in the fall. The job is mine if I want it."

She tucked her hair behind her ear. "Are you interested in taking it?"

"That depends on a tearoom owner I know."

A slight frown marred her brow, and J.C. stopped breathing.

"What if..." She caught her bottom lip between her teeth. "What if you give up your job in Chicago and things don't...work out...between us?"

"Do you expect that to happen?"

"No. But the Anderson women don't have a good track record with men."

"I plan to be the exception. But if by some chance

things don't go as I hope they do, I'll find a job somewhere else. Cops are always in demand. And for the record, I want you to know I'm not rushing you. We'll take as long as we need to be certain. I just want to make sure you're willing to give this a chance and see where it leads."

A slow smile warmed Heather's face, dispelling J.C.'s fears as surely as the sun chases away the fog on a Nantucket morning.

"I've never been much of a gambler…but I have a feeling this time the odds are in my favor. Take the job, J.C."

Returning her smile, he lifted her hand to his lips and pressed a kiss to her fingers. "I'll express my feelings on this subject more thoroughly after dinner."

And two hours later, as they strolled hand in hand along a bluff above the beach toward her car, as a canopy of stars twinkled above them, as a rising moon turned the sea to silver, he kept his promise.

Epilogue

Five months later

"So where are we going?"

At Heather's question, J.C. gave her a quick grin before turning his attention back to the road. "It's a surprise. Are you ready for your family to descend for the holidays?"

"You're changing the subject."

"Guilty. But humor me, okay? I'll make it worth your while."

"That sounds like a bribe."

Mock horror suffused his face. "From a cop? Never."

Shooting him a disgruntled look, she folded her arms across her chest. "You aren't going to budge, are you?"

"Nope."

Giving up, she settled back in the seat and

cracked her window, enjoying the sixty-two-degree temperature and the cloudless blue sky, which made it feel more like spring than mid-December. The unseasonably warm weather, in fact, was what had prompted this unexpected outing. J.C. had come knocking at her door half an hour ago, and using that cajoling smile she loved, he'd persuaded her to set aside her baking for a few hours and take advantage of the glorious day.

It had not been a hard sell.

She took a deep breath of the fresh air. "To answer your question, yes, I'm ready for my family. Susan and Brian are arriving three days before Christmas. Dad's coming a week early. He told me this morning that the latest MRI was fine."

"That's great news." J.C. turned off on the road to Bartlett's Farm.

She grinned. "Okay. I've got it. We're going to get some macaroons, right?"

"Nope. I had some good news this morning, too. Marci's going to ace this semester despite working full-time. And Nathan expects to finish his GED by summer."

Though his tone was casual, Heather heard the pride in his voice. And the contentment. Such a change from the early days of their relationship, she reflected, when worry about his brother and anguish over the drug bust had etched his features with dejection and grief.

"It sounds like everything is falling into place with your family, too."

"Just about. I only have one more detail to work out."

Before she could query him about that comment, he passed Bartlett's Farm and turned onto an unpaved road. Her eyebrows rose in surprise. "Are we going to Ladies Beach?"

"Yep." The undercurrent of excitement in his single-word response and the half smile playing at his lips sent a tingle of excitement zipping through her.

Something was up.

A few minutes later, she caught sight of a uniformed Todd standing beside a police car, arms folded across his chest as he gazed out to sea. Like a sentinel.

When he saw them approaching, he lifted his hand in greeting, rounded the car and slid into the driver's seat. As he passed, he grinned and gave a thumbs-up.

"What was that all about?" Heather swiveled her head to watch him drive away.

Instead of answering, J.C. pulled close to where Todd had been parked, set the brake and shut off the engine. "Your questions are about to be answered. Sit tight until I come around."

She did as he asked, waiting while he lifted the trunk lid, then slammed it shut. When he pulled her door open, he was holding a wicker basket.

"We're having a picnic on the beach? In December?"

"Why not? I can't think of a better place to celebrate."

She climbed out of the car and stood beside him. "What are we celebrating?"

Taking her hand, he walked her over to the edge of the bluff and positioned her toward the sea.

Heather stopped breathing.

Below her, a giant heart had been drawn in the sand. In the center were the words *Will you be mine?* Beside it a small lean-to had been erected, a towel spread on the sand inside it, a fire burning in a small grate in front of it.

"I've been waiting three weeks for a nice enough day to do this."

At J.C.'s husky confession, Heather turned toward him. The warmth in his eyes was more than sufficient to dispel the slight chill from the ocean breeze.

Setting the basket on the sand, he took her hands in his strong, lean fingers, and his eyes softened with tenderness. "These past few months have been the happiest of my life, Heather. I didn't come to Nantucket looking for romance, but God surprised me. He put you in my life—and I can't imagine spending the rest of it without you. I love you more than I thought it was possible to love anyone." He inclined his head toward the beach and swallowed. Hard. "I think I've already tipped my hand, but…would you do me the honor of becoming my wife?"

Joy spilled out of her heart, suffusing her entire

body with radiant warmth. "I can't imagine spending the rest of my life without you, either."

"Is that a yes?"

"Do I need to spell it out?"

He grinned. "That would be nice."

Grinning, she tugged her hands free and scrambled down to the beach, grabbing a stick en route. Trotting over to the giant heart, she drew a smaller one beside it. Inside, she wrote one word.

Yes!!!

Tossing the stick aside, she planted her hands on her hips and grinned up at him. "Good enough?"

Instead of responding, he snagged the picnic basket, descended to the beach and took her in his arms. "Not until we seal it with a kiss."

He leaned toward her, but she pulled back. "Wait. I have one question. What if this nice weather hadn't happened on a day when the tearoom was closed?"

A smug smile lifted his lips. "Edith was going to fill in after I spirited you away on some excuse."

Heather chuckled. Being clued in to the proposal would have been the proverbial icing on the cake for the Lighthouse Lane matchmaker.

"Why do I think there will be a message on my answering machine when I get home, offering me some sort of sweet treat?"

J.C. smiled. "There's only one sweet treat that interests me at the moment."

He pulled her close, into the shelter of his arms,

and as the pounding of the surf mingled with the pounding of her heart, she gave thanks.

For this special man, who had taught her to trust—and to hope.

For new beginnings.

And for the gift of true love. The kind that endured, undimmed by adversity.

The kind J.C. had offered her.

For always.

* * * * *

Dear Reader,

Welcome back to LIGHTHOUSE LANE!

When I envisioned this series, I knew The Devon Rose would play a prominent role in one of the books. What I didn't envision was a romance between genteel Heather, who inhabits the rarified world of high tea, and J.C., a street-savvy undercover cop who's used to the gritty side of life. But as these two characters came alive for me, I discovered they were perfect for each other. I hope you enjoy watching them make that discovery, too!

To learn more about my books, I invite you to visit my Web site at www.irenehannon.com. Watch for Marci's story, coming next in my LIGHTHOUSE LANE series.

In the meantime, I wish all of you a wonderful summer!

Irene Hannon

QUESTIONS FOR DISCUSSION

1. J.C. believes he's failed to keep the promise he made to his mother to take care of his two siblings. Do you think he should feel guilty about this? Why or why not? Have you ever made a promise that you weren't able to keep? How did you deal with that?

2. When her parents separate, Heather cuts all contact with her father, blaming him for the destruction of their family. In this story, however, she learns new information that makes her regret that decision. Have you ever followed a course of action out of anger or stubbornness and later regretted it? How did that affect your life? What does the Bible teach us on this subject?

3. J.C. blames himself for the death of his colleagues, assuming he made a mistake that cost them their lives. What advice would you give him to help him cope with his guilt? Have you ever made a mistake that had negative repercussions? How did you deal with it? What role did your faith play?

4. Order, predictability and control were important to Heather. Why? Was this healthy? Why or why not?

5. Infidelity has affected all of the Anderson women. Talk about this problem and how it impacts relationships. Why is it one of the hardest mistakes to forgive? Can trust be rebuilt in a relationship after a partner cheats? If so, what would it take to get a relationship back on track?

6. When J.C. arrives on Nantucket, Heather wants no part of him. Identify some of the things he does that convince her he's a man worth loving and trusting.

7. After his parents' break up, Heather's nephew is angry and he starts down a dangerous path. Discuss some of the destructive behavior he exhibits. Have you ever had to deal with destructive behavior in a teen? How did you address it?

8. When Heather's father is diagnosed with a brain tumor, he pays her an unannounced visit, setting a reunion in motion. Why does it often take a life-threatening emergency for people to rethink long-held positions? What lessons do such situations teach us that we should apply to our normal, everyday lives?

9. The news that the drug bust ambush was the result of information provided by his brother dis-

heartens J.C. Yet he doesn't want to believe he was deliberately set up because he still holds out hope of a reconciliation. Have you ever persevered in loving someone despite rejection? Why?

10. After he learns about the repercussions of the information he provided, Nathan tries to take his life. Talk about suicide, and the reasons people consider it. What is the best way to deal with someone who has lost hope?

11. When J.C. arrives at the prison, he is presented with the dog-eared, much-read letters he'd sent to Nathan. What does this say about the power of love? Share some examples of redemptive or transforming love from your own life.

12. Near the end of the story, J.C. tells Heather about his Nantucket job offer and asks her if she wants him to stay. Do you think she was wise to be cautious? Why or why not?

13. At the beginning of the book, Heather and J.C. seem like an unlikely couple. How do they each change during the course of the story in ways that open the door to a relationship? Talk about a change, growth experience or insight you've had in your life that set you on a new path.

*A thrilling romance between a British nurse
and an American cowboy on the African plains.*

*Turn the page for a sneak preview of
THE MAVERICK'S BRIDE
by Catherine Palmer.
Available September 2009
from Love Inspired® Historical.*

Adam hoisted himself onto the balcony, swinging one leg at a time over the rail. He hoped he hadn't been spotted by a compound guard.

But the sight of Emma Pickering peering out from behind the curtain put his concerns to rest. He had done the right thing.

"Good morning, Miss Pickering." He leaned against the white window frame.

"Mr. King." She was almost breathless. "I cannot speak with you."

"But I need to talk. Mind if I come inside?"

"Indeed, sir, you may not take another step! Are you mad?"

He couldn't hold back a grin. "No more than most. I figure anyone who would leave home and travel all the way to Africa has to be a little off-kilter."

"You refer to me, I suppose? I'll have you know I'm here for a very good reason."

"Railway inspection, is it? Or nursing?"

Emma looked even better than he had thought she might—and he had thought about her a lot.

"Speaking of nursing," he ventured.

"Mr. King, I have already told you I'm unavailable. Now please let yourself down by that...that rope thing, and—"

"My lasso?"

"You must go down again, sir. This is unseemly."

Emma was edgy this morning. Almost frightened. Different from the bold young woman he had met yesterday.

He couldn't let that concern him. Last night after he left the consulate, he had made up his mind to keep things strictly business with Emma Pickering.

"I'll leave after I've had my say," he told her. "This is important."

"Speak quickly, sir. My father must not find you here."

"With all due respect, Emma, do you think I'm concerned about what your father thinks?"

"You may not care, but I do. What do you want from me?"

"I need a nurse."

"A nurse? Are you ill?"

"Not for me. I have a friend—at my ranch."

Her eyes deepened in concern as she let the curtain drop a little. "What sort of illness does your friend have? Can you describe it?"

Adam looked away. How could he explain the situation without scaring her off?

"It's not an illness. It's more like..."

Searching for the right words, he turned back to Emma. But at the first full sight of her face, he reached through the open window and pulled the curtain out of her hands.

"Emma, what happened to you?" He caught her arm and drew her toward him. "Who did this?"

She raised her hand in a vain effort to cover her cheek and eye. "It's nothing," she protested, trying to back away. "Please, Mr. King, you must not…"

Even as she tried to speak, he stepped through the balcony door and gathered her into his arms. Brushing back the hair from her cheek, he noted the swelling and the darkening stain around it.

"Emma," he growled. "Who did this to you?"

She fell motionless, silent in his embrace. No wonder she had shied like a scared colt. She hadn't wanted him to know.

Torn with dismay that anyone would ever harm this beautiful woman, he felt an irresistible urge to kiss her.

"Emma, you have to tell me…." Realization flooded through him. A pompous, nattily dressed English railroad tycoon had struck his own daughter.

"Leave me, I beg you. You have no place here."

"Emma, wait. Listen to me." Adam caught her wrists and pulled her back toward him. He'd never been a man to think things through too carefully. He did what felt right.

"I want you to come with me," he told her. "I need

your help. Let's go right now. Emma, I'll take care of you."

"I don't need anyone to take care of me," she shot back. "God is watching over me."

"Emma!" Both turned toward the open door where Emma's sister stood, eyes wide.

"Emma, go with him!" Cissy crossed the room toward them. "Run away with him, Emma. It's your chance to escape—to become a nurse, as you've always wanted. You'll be safe at last, and you can have your dream."

Emma turned back to Adam.

"Come on," he urged her. "Let's get moving."

* * * * *

*Will Emma run away with Adam and finally
realize her dreams of becoming a nurse?
Find out in THE MAVERICK'S BRIDE,
available in September 2009
only from Love Inspired® Historical.*

Love Inspired® SUSPENSE

RIVETING INSPIRATIONAL ROMANCE

These contemporary tales
of intrigue and romance
feature Christian characters
facing challenges to their faith...
and their lives!

**Four new Love Inspired Suspense titles are
available every month wherever books are
sold, including most bookstores, supermarkets,
drug stores and discount stores.**

Steeple
Hill®

Visit:
www.steeplehillbooks.com

Love Inspired.
HISTORICAL
INSPIRATIONAL HISTORICAL ROMANCE

Engaging stories of romance,
adventure and faith,
these novels are set in
various historical periods
from biblical times
to World War II.

NOW AVAILABLE!

**Steeple
Hill®**